Also available in Large Print
by Anne Morice:

Death and the Dutiful Daughter
Getting Away with Murder
Murder Post-Dated

Dead on Cue

Anne Morice

G.K.HALL &CO.
Boston, Massachusetts
1986

Published in Large Print by arrangement with
St. Martin's Press.

G.K. Hall Large Print Book Series.

Set in 16 pt. Plantin.

Library of Congress Cataloging in Publication Data

Morice, Anne.
  Dead on cue.

  (G.K. Hall large print book series)
  1. Large type books.   I. Title.
[PR6063.O743D39   1986]   823'.914   86-14284
ISBN 0-8161-4118-5 (lg. print)

Dead on Cue

1

'Ever heard of the Alibi Club?,' Robin asked when he was driving me home after one of the most disastrous first nights in theatrical history.

'No, never. It sounds more up your street than mine.'

'The sort of club that provides false alibis at cut prices to members who get into bad odour with Scotland Yard, you mean? Yes, I daresay there are a few of those knocking around, but this is quite different. Eminently respectable, in fact. The membership is restricted to forty and they're all top flight mystery writers. It started with a bunch of old fashioned classic detective novelists, but they're getting thinner on the ground now, so the umbrella's been extended to include science fiction and so on. They have no premises of their own, but they meet informally four times a year for dinner in some

Soho restaurant, whose name for the moment escapes me.'

'But what gave you the idea that I would know anything about it? Or were you just pulling any old subject out of the air to take my mind off the current tragedy in my life?'

'Well, that too, I suppose, but this happens to be one which has been very much on my own mind for some time now. I haven't mentioned it before because, what with dress rehearsals and previews and raving hysteria, which have set the pattern of our daily lives just recently, there has hardly been an opportunity. And the reason why I thought you might have heard of it was that your old friend, William Montgomerie, had been a member for over twenty years.'

'It's stretching it a bit to refer to him as my old friend. I only met him half a dozen times and we never discussed anything much except the script and how he saw the character I was playing. I didn't even know whether he was married until I read the obituary.'

'All the same, you liked and admired him, did you not?'

'Very much. It was a marvellous script and I had a wonderful part in it. What more could one ask from any writer? I can imagine he might have been a terror in the home, though. He was a prima donna of a perfectionist, for a start, which always makes impossible demands on other people. Single-minded and egocentric, too. I daresay that applies to a good many writers.'

'Maybe, I wouldn't know. Was he married?'

'Twice. He was divorced from his first wife and I don't know what became of her. The following year he married Gwen somebody or other, who survives him.'

'What a memory!'

'Well, it was only a few months after we'd finished filming, so naturally I was interested. What is all this leading up to, by the way? Is there some rumour now going round that he did not die from natural causes and you've had orders to make a few discreet enquiries?'

'Far from it. I was simply hoping that, having known Montgomerie personally and got on so well with him, you might be able to tell me something I ought to know about the members of the Alibi Club.'

'Why? What have they ever done to you?'

'Something rather dreadful. They have

invited me to speak at their next dinner, on the twenty-third of this month.'

'No! Have they really? But how marvellous! Can it mean that you're becoming a celebrity and I hadn't even noticed?'

'God forbid. One of those in the family is quite enough. Also, when I said they'd invited me, I was laying it on a bit. What happened was that our revered Assistant Commissioner had been dragooned into being their guest of honour on this occasion, but a week ago he discovered, to his immense relief, no doubt, that it clashed with some official function which took priority, so he was able to slide out gracefully. Asked to suggest a substitute from among the underlings, he had the bright idea of putting me up for it and I daresay it would not enhance my chances of promotion if I were to refuse.'

'And why should you want to? But what's all this talk about speeches and guests of honour? I thought you said these dinners were informal?'

'As a rule, they are, but every so often, as with this one, they all dress up in their best shrouds and put on a gala occasion to welcome the new member.'

'Willie's death having created a vacancy, of course. Am I invited?'

'You most certainly are. I have a strong suspicion that you are really to blame for this awful prospect which now hangs over me. The A.C., correctly no doubt, reckoned that my charm and personality might not be enough to draw the crowds, but with Theresa Crichton in tow I should get by. I've gone so far as to interpolate a few remarks in my speech about your being such a dedicated crime fiction addict, which should do me a bit of good, but I had to explain to Nigel Banks, who is the President, that in fact he will have to find an understudy for you, as next Thursday week you will be engaged elsewhere.'

'Which turns out to have been over-optimistic. If the reviews are half as bad as I expect them to be, I shall be out of work long before Thursday week.'

'Well, that wouldn't be all bad, from my point of view, although I hope for your sake that you're now being over-pessimistic.'

'Thank you, Robin. I hope so too, although it might be fun to change roles for once. This time I should be the one to sit looking nonchalant and composed, with my hands clenched under the table, in case you forget your lines or start sneezing just as you reach the climax.'

'Are you suggesting that's the kind of torment I go through when I'm watching you?'

'Do you deny it?'

'Not entirely, but I believe I am getting hardened at last. And I'd swop it any day of the week for having to be the one to stand up and make an ass of myself in public.'

This was not quite the style in which I would have chosen to hear my artistic endeavours described, but I reminded myself that it was most likely destined to sound like flattery, compared to the insults which were even now being sharpened up in time for the morning editions.

He did not sneeze or forget his lines. On the contrary, his twelve minute speech was delivered with almost professional grace and timing, which was just as it should have been, three days of unemployment having enabled me to put him through a remorseless rehearsal course.

Prominent among those who came up to congratulate him, after the vote of thanks from the President, was an elderly woman wearing what appeared to be a purple silk tent. She was large and straight-backed, with Grecian features and lots of dyed red hair, and had she been auditioning for the part of Cleopatra's grandmother during a stormy period of her life, she would have got it without opening her mouth. Her luminous dark eyes were huge and tragic, but the corners of her mouth kept turning up in a catlike smile of irresistible humour and charm.

'This is the time when we're allowed to move around amongst ourselves,' she explained, taking a cigarette case and lighter from her matching purple bag, 'so I've come to grab my place opposite the guests of honour before anyone else gets a look-in. Nigel is lining up far more important people than me for the privilege, but, as I'm such an old, old member now, he feels bound to overlook my pushy ways. I'm Myrtle Sprygge, by the way.'

'Oh, my goodness, are you really?' I asked, cheered by this news, since it was a name that even Robin might have heard of. 'How wonderful to meet you! We're both terrific fans. You remember Robin? All those lovely books about that wildly attractive man called Peter, who's a professor of oriental studies and solves every puzzle by asking himself how Confucius would have handled it. Do tell me, Miss Sprygge, I've always wondered, have you spent much time in China? I suppose you must have, otherwise it wouldn't sound nearly so convincing.'

I rattled on in this vein for a minute or two, giving Robin time to dredge about in his memory, although without much success, it appeared, for when it came to his turn to contribute something to the conversation he confined himself to asking whether she was currently at work on a new novel.

'Alas, no, I have quite given up writing these days. Or rather, as the saying goes, it has given me up. It is five years now since anything of mine was published.'

'How dreadful for you!' I sighed. 'Just five days without work has been enough to make me jittery.'

'Perhaps you have too many other things to do to find time for writing?' Robin suggested, although he was tactful enough not to add: 'like looking after your house and husband, for instance.'

'No, my dear, I can't pretend that's true. It's pure laziness, if you must know. I'm bone idle and I've been discovering how comfortable laurels are to rest on.'

The last remark had been overheard by Nigel Banks, the President, who had now re-seated himself on my left, having completed his tour of the other tables, and he leant across to her, saying:

'You'll have to go back to your own chair and rest on them there now, Myrtle. The ceremony is about to begin.'

He was a russet coloured man, with bristly hair and moustache, resembling something between a fox and a gamekeeper, and he would probably have looked more at home in a knickerbocker suit than a dinner jacket. I had been told that he regularly published two or three novels a year, using four different pseudonyms, as nowadays it did not do for a writer to be too prolific. It had made me realise how fortunate Dickens and Trollope were not to have been troubled by such niceties of public prejudice.

'If you say so, darling', Myrtle replied, gathering her tent around her and rising majestically to her feet. Then, looking down at me, she added in a low voice: 'Don't run away afterwards, Theresa Crichton. There is something very special I wish to ask you.'

Without waiting for an answer, she gave me a peremptory two-fingered tap on the shoulder and walked away.

Watching her go, Mr Banks picked up a fork and, with a gesture not dissimilar to hers, rapped on a plate for silence before beginning to speak:

'Honoured guests, ladies and gentlemen: I know that all members here tonight will be especially conscious of the great loss we have suffered in the death of our old friend and colleague, Willie Montgomerie, but I think I can say with confidence that he would have approved whole-heartedly of the choice which the committee has arrived at unanimously of his successor and our latest addition to this honourable company. I feel I could have no surer endorsement of this belief than Gwen having agreed to join us tonight for this special occasion. So now, without more ado, allow me to present to you our new member, Leslie Bockmer.'

When the applause was over and the President had followed up with a résumé of the new member's literary achievements, Mr Bockmer, who had been sitting mute and almost invisible on the President's left during dinner, stood up, cleared his throat and muttered something on the lines of 'Ta very much.'

As it happened, he was scarcely more visible when standing than sitting, being not much over five feet tall, of mild and unremarkable appearance and with a manner betraying shyness, bordering at this moment on panic.

As a dedicated student of psychology, I was riveted by this performance, for I had read some of the Bockmer novels and in each of them the hero had been the same tall, extrovert man of the world, loping around with manly strides and nerves of steel and with every young woman in sight prostrating herself at his feet. Not for the first time that evening, it brought home to me how fortunate in some respects authors were, compared to actors. If he had been on the stage, it must have been poor Mr Bockmer's lot to have been typecast as an insignificant, comically shy man, so condemning him to a life quite devoid of variety. Whereas the profession he had so wisely chosen enabled him to act out his secret fantasies during every minute of his working

11

life and thereby earn enough money to carry on doing so.

I was so absorbed in these reflections and in studying the subject of them that I failed to notice what had led to the subdued fracas which was now taking place at the far end of the room. All I could see was an over-turned chair and a man with white hair standing up and signalling to a waiter. There also appeared to be another man and two women on their knees on the floor.

Fortunately, Robin had been more alert and when Mr Banks had left us to go and investigate, he leant across the gap between us and said in an undertone:

'Is that what they call slaying them in the aisles? I suppose the excitement of meeting you was too much for her.'

'You mean something has happened to Myrtle Sprygge?'

'Fainted dead away, as far as I could make out. Everything appeared to be perfectly normal and then she just keeled over and subsided gracefully on to the floor.'

Like everyone else, we had been keeping our eyes glued to this scene and now watched in silence as the two men, after a conference which included Mr Banks, managed with some difficulty to raise the recumbent Myrtle and, with one at each end, to carry her out of the door which the waiter was holding open for them.

'Sorry about that,' the President said, returning to his seat and looking ruddier and more bristly than ever.

'What happened?' I asked. 'Did she faint?'

Before replying, he glanced at Robin, jerking his elbow upwards in a man-to-man gesture:

'No, she'll be all right, she's had these turns before. Luckily, James Ormsby, one of the chaps who carted her out, is a doctor in his other life and he says there's nothing to worry about. Soon as she's on her feet, he's going to see her home. Now then, how about another brandy to round off the evening?'

'No, thanks,' Robin said. 'After such splendid hospitality, it might be wiser to leave before we have to be carried out too. Goodnight and many thanks. It has been a most interesting and enjoyable evening.'

'It was too, don't you think?' he asked, as we went down in the lift. 'A pity the curtain had to come down just before the end. Still,

I don't see that the A.C. can blame me for that, do you?'

'I feel sorry about Myrtle,' I remarked when we were back at home in Beacon Square, 'I rather took to her and I'd been looking forward to hearing whatever it was she wanted to ask me. Incidentally, she seemed sober enough then, didn't she? It must have caught up with her very suddenly.'

'Oh, you can't tell. Some people manage to carry their drink gracefully right up to the moment when they pass out. They seem to go from sobriety to unconsciousness in one short step. Or are you hinting that someone may have slipped a knockout dose into her brandy glass? If so, I imagine William Montgomerie's widow would be your favourite candidate for that job, since they were sitting next to each other.'

'How do you know they were? Did Mr Banks tell you?'

'No, it was my own deduction. Like you, I was rather taken with Myrtle. She certainly stood out in the crowd and I was watching her and the other people at her table during the speeches. When it came to the bit about thanking Gwen for coming, I

14

noticed a small incident. You did tell me that the second Mrs Montgomerie was called Gwen, as I recall, so obviously that's who he was referring to.'

'What was the incident?'

'The woman sitting next to Myrtle bowed her head and dabbed her eyes with a napkin. Then the man on her other side, the white-haired one, covered her other hand with his own and gave it a sort of sympathetic squeeze. From all of which I deduced that the eye dabber was the deceased member's widow.'

'And I'd say you deduced right. What did she look like?'

'Unremarkable. Rather pretty, in a dim sort of way. She must have been a good bit younger than her husband, though. In her thirties, I should imagine.'

'Young enough to be his daughter, in that case. Willie was sixty-four when he died.'

'Was it sudden, or had he been ill for some time?'

'Not as far as I know. He was always bursting with vitality, whenever I saw him. Very dynamic too and he was a terrific worker. Most likely dropped down with a heart attack.'

'Oh, surely you're not going to be satisfied with anything so tame?'

'Now what are you insinuating?'

'It occurred to me that now that you find yourself so unexpectedly at a loose end you'd be looking for something to occupy your time till the next job comes along. What better than a situation like this to get to grips with? It has all the classic ingredients which anyone with your turn of mind could ask for. Young wife, tied to a much older man, bored to tears because, far from treating her like a baby doll, he devotes all his energies to work. Then there's the financial aspect to consider too, isn't there? Presumably, his novels will go on being reprinted for all eternity, so she'll be quite well off. Aren't you tempted to enquire a little further into this unexpected but timely death?'

Rising to the bait, I said: 'To hear you talk, anyone might imagine that one of my objects in life has been to go around creating criminals and crimes for them to commit. Perhaps you secretly believe that no thoughts of murder would have entered those people's heads if I hadn't planted them there? If so, allow me to say that you are mistaken. I consider it far more likely that more evil deeds are committed daily under the noses of the police than are dreamt of in your philosophy. Perhaps you are all too busy lugging protesters about and going to community relations courses to have time any more for the old fashioned crimes, but it seems to me that anyone of average intelligence could easily contrive and carry out the murder of someone living at close quarters and, if it weren't for interfering amateurs like myself, most of them would get away with it.'

'That's my girl!' Robin said, looking smug about it.

2

Needless to say, I had no intention of busying myself in the matter of Willie's death, which, after the initial shock, had scarcely affected me. Luckily, he had produced more than forty crime novels in his time, about half of which I had not yet read, and it was these, much more than the life and death of their author, which interested me.

Not being blessed with second sight, no warning voice intruded upon this comfortable state of affairs when, two days after the Alibi Club dinner, Myrtle Sprygge telephoned to invite me to lunch.

It was unexpected however, and I regarded it as a sign of rare mental and physical resilience that neither my existence nor the memory of having something special to say to me had been blotted out by the fact that ten minutes after expressing it she had collapsed in a drunken stupor.

'I expect it was just that President being spiteful,' Robin said, when I drew his attention to this phenomenon. 'Rather a bitten-up sort of character, I thought, and I daresay the poor woman suffers from epilepsy or diabetes. Did you accept?'

'Had to. She asked me to choose my own day. Any one I like between now and next Christmas was what it amounted to, so there was no getting out of it. Not that I wanted to, as it happens. I rather liked that weird Myrtle and I'm curious to know what she's so keen to talk to me about. I expect it will only turn out to be an idea she's got for a television series, but you never know.'

She lived within five minutes walk of Swiss Cottage, in a gloomy Victorian House, which had been converted into five self-contained flats. Hers had started life as the basement, but had now become the garden flat. It consisted of a bedroom and bathroom and one enormous room at the back, which served as kitchen, dining room, workroom and study, with a television set at one end and an up-to-date version of a kitchen range at the other.

In the centre of the outside wall there was

a door on to a narrow paved terrace, sheltered on its further side by a high bank, with steps cut into it, up to the garden proper. This too was on a miniature scale, which may have been just as well, because it had been sadly neglected and even the weeds looked unhealthy and dejected.

'A bit cramped, isn't it?' Myrtle said, looking round the room. 'I've tried to cram in too much, but then that's the story of my life. On the other hand, it suits me down to the ground, to bring out a well tried pun. Just big enough to hold everything I need and practically no stairs. I have to think about boring things like that nowadays. Can't even clamber up to the top deck of a bus any more.'

'Why's that?' I asked, thinking that she didn't look all that old and a little clambering might have done something to bring her weight down.

'Groggy ticker, my dear. Have to be careful, you know. What an awful fate! Shall we have drinks outside before I fling the lunch together? Alcohol is one of the few remaining pleasures in life which hasn't been totally vetoed, so far. I don't suppose I'd pay much attention, if it were. There is such a thing as being too careful.'

'I'm sorry about your heart, though. Is it serious?'

'Not so long as I behave myself, do everything the doctors tell me, nothing to excess and don't get over-excited. As excess is my middle name and there are very few things in life I can't get over-excited about, given half a chance, I find it all very frustrating. However, you catch me at a favourable moment. I'm toeing all the lines at present. That tiresome charade you may have witnessed at the club dinner was a timely warning. I gather it broke the party up, but I don't feel specially bad about that. You'd probably had enough by then anyway and your adorable husband's speech was the only bright spot. The rest was rather dire, don't you think? And I shall never understand what possessed the Committee to elect that frumpy little Bockmer person. I can't see him adding much sparkle to our dinners and I should imagine Willie must be turning in his grave. Or turning in his urn, I suppose one should say.'

I could find several remarks worthy of comment in this speech, but decided to take a leaf from Robin's book and begin at the beginning:

'We were sorry the evening had to end the way it did, but at least you seem to have recovered quite quickly.'

'Oh yes, I have all the right pills you know and Gwen was a brick. Helped me to bed and insisted on spending the night on the sofa. Still, that's often the way, isn't it?'

'Often what way?'

'Oh, you know, the people you haven't much time for as you go sailing through life are so often the ones who come steaming up to the rescue when your boat capsizes. Rather chastening, really. Haven't you found that?'

'Yes, frequently, but I don't let it chasten me. I think they get a tremendous thrill out of it.'

'Oh, thank you, my dear, I am sure you are right and you have made me feel much better. I knew we should get on well.'

She was gabbling a bit and I began to suspect that she had either, after all, forgotten there was something particular she wanted to say to me, or that second thoughts had prevailed in the interval. I was wrong, though, because during lunch—which, flung together notwithstanding, was on the gourmet level—she revealed what had all the while been on her mind.

'How well did you know Willie?' she began by asking.

'Not well at all. We worked together before and during the rehearsals and shooting and I saw a lot of him then, but I'd never met him before and I never saw him again afterwards.'

'Yes, he told me about it and quite a lot about you, incidentally. Knowing him as I did, I'm damn sure that during those few weeks you became the most important woman in his life and the one he would have been most ready to confide in. The fact that he could have passed you in the street six months later without recognising you is neither here nor there. It would simply indicate that he had become engrossed in some new project and that his life now revolved round someone else. There was never room for more than one at a time.'

'I'm sure you're right, Myrtle, but you shouldn't assume that he ever confided in me on a personal level. Our relationship was strictly professional.'

'I don't doubt it my dear, and it is precisely what I had been hoping to hear. It would have been no use to me if he had fallen for your beautiful blue eyes. He was more than capable of doing so, but in that case he would have talked of nothing but them and the strange fascination you exerted over him. No use at all. What I am interested to know is whether during those long sessions together he discussed his work? Work in general, I mean, not just that particular script?'

'Sometimes he did, yes.'

'And the work of other writers too, perhaps?'

'Yes, they cropped up occasionally.'

'Myself?'

'Among others, yes. He was a great admirer of yours, as I'm sure you know. He specially praised the economy of your writing and what he described as your marvellous ear for dialogue. He once gave it as his opinion that you would have been a natural for the theatre.'

'Which is nice to hear and I know he meant it too. He encouraged me from the beginning. In fact, it was all due to him that I took it up in the first place. I must assure you, though, Theresa Crichton, that I am not subjecting you to this tiresome inquisition in order to hear my own praises. There is something specific which I badly need to find out and you may be able to help me. I suppose Willie didn't happen to mention that he was, or had been, reading the draft of a new novel which I had asked him to look at?'

'Not that I recall. Didn't he tell you himself?'

'I sent it to him a few months before he died. He had asked me to and normally he was meticulous about passing on his criticisms and suggestions in double quick time, but with this one he rang me up two or three days after I had sent the manuscript and asked me to be patient. He had been invited to collaborate on an adaptation of one of his novels for television. It was the first time he'd taken on anything of that kind and he could tell it was going to be very time consuming. He had no intention of breaking his promise, but I must understand and forgive him, if I didn't hear from him for several weeks.'

'But you never heard at all? Is that it?'

'Not about that. He became ill soon afterwards.'

'I can see how frustrating that must have

been for you, but was it so desperately important? After all, you're very well known and your books have been selling like hot cakes since . . . .'

'Since you were in your pram. I know, but that's not the point.'

'Isn't it? I should have expected it to have given you enough confidence to know by now whether something you'd written was good or not, without having it confirmed by the guru?'

'All very true. Willie could still be an enormous help, but I could have got along well enough without him. Sending the first rough draft had become a ritual, almost a superstition, you might say, like always using one special pen and having everything on your desk arranged in the same pattern. However, that's not really the point either. I have a very particular reason for wanting to know what became of this one, which has nothing to do with its literary merit.'

'So what has it to do with?'

'I need to know whether he read it and, more important, whether anyone else read it. What became of it, in short, after it tumbled through his letter box all those months ago. Gwen doesn't know. She has sorted through all his papers, which was probably the work of a moment, I might add, since Joyce kept everything in apple pie order. There isn't even the usual worry about what to keep and what to throw away because under the terms of his will every scrap of correspondence, diaries and stuff like that, goes into the archives of some American university, who will gobble it up with howls of joy. The only exceptions were such papers and manuscripts which the two literary executors decided rightly belonged elsewhere. Gwen assures me these did not include anything of mine.'

'Who are the literary executors?'

'Gwen herself and Joyce Harman, Willie's secretary, who worked for him for years. Did you not meet her?'

'No, but I believe I did once speak to her on the telephone.'

'A very formidable old party and far too efficient and conscientious to have been guilty of an oversight of that kind. So there it is. It is inconceivable that Willie would have destroyed it and my only hope is to try and extend the search. Always the romantic optimist, I had this mental picture of you and Willie at your table for two in the studio canteen and Willie saying: "I wish you'd cast an eye over this some time and see what you think of it. I shan't tell you who wrote it because you'd recognise the name and that might prejudice you." Not a true picture, I gather?'

'Sorry, no. Was it the only copy?'

'Yes, although that has no importance now either. The first thing I shall do, if I ever do get it back, is to throw it straight into that old monster of a stove.'

'Oh, really? Then what . . . ?'

'Is all the fuss about? I shall tell you. You have been so patient with me that an explanation is the least you deserve. And I feel I deserve better than to be dismissed as a poor, crazed old woman, which is probably how you see me at this minute. It's a long story though, and it goes back several years, so I shall bring the cheese and fruit and pour you another glass of wine before I start. Forgive me if I don't join you. I warned you that this was to be one of my careful days.'

Myrtle had not overestimated the chances of being dismissed as a crazed old woman because, when she got to it at last, her explanation began with yet another question.

'What do you know about the circumstances of Willie's death?'

'Nothing whatever, except that it must have been rather sudden.'

'Sudden, yes, but not altogether unexpected. There is a difference. However, that's jumping ahead and first, as I warned you, I have to go back a few years. Seven, to be exact. Do you know America well?'

'Only bits of it,' I replied, wondering if she really was off her head.

'That puts you ahead of me at your age. Curiously enough, I never set foot on those shores until I was in my sixties. The war had something to do with it, of course. I have dozens of friends over there who've all entreated me to go and stay with them, but somehow or other it never seemed to be the right moment. Then, seven years ago, I'd just finished a novel, I was no longer married by then and I felt ready for a change of scene, so off I went for four whole weeks.'

'And did it come up to your expectations?'

'Surpassed them, my dear. Best thing I ever did, I said to myself. At the time, that is. Afterwards, I began to wonder if it hadn't been a great mistake. If I'd stayed quietly at home, I might have gone on for years, writing my harmless little books and growing old gracefully. I might never have discovered the curse that had been laid upon me.'

'Oh, goodness, what was that?'

'That I was a witch.'

Members of my profession become accustomed to hearing some odd confessions from time to time, but this one was outside my experience and I could find nothing at all to say, a vacuum which allowed Myrtle to come leaping in with another question:

'Do you remember my telling your lovely husband that writing had given me up, instead of the other way round?'

I nodded and she went on: 'That was just the routine excuse. Not true. I often wish it was. The truth is that there've been three novels since that New York trip, two completed, one not, but I haven't been able to publish any of them.'

'Because of being a witch? I think I'd have expected that to be more of a help than a hindrance.'

'In my case, it has worked against me. I told you that I had a new book all wrapped up and on its way to the printers when I left for America? While I was over there I spent a few days with a friend who was living in Vermont, and still does, for all I know. She was in the rag trade and I used to see a lot of her when she came to Europe for the fashion shows and all that caper. During my visit she told me a very sad story. I shall now endeavour to curb my natural loquacity and repeat it to you in shortened form. Her name is Martha and she is a few years younger than me. Her marriage turned out badly and she and her husband have been separated since before I met her. There were no children, but she did not regret this because she has always put her career first. She led a full and interesting life, surrounded by friends and with one very special companion. His name was Teddy and he was also divorced. I can't tell you how their friendship began, but they had known and loved each other, in their detached way, for many years. When Teddy retired and appearances no longer mattered he and Martha set up house together. Each of them had enough to live on and they simply pooled their resources. Martha's capital consisted of savings from her vast income during her career and Teddy had insured his life for a hefty sum, in favour of his daughter, to whom he also paid a monthly allowance from income. She was his only child and was married to a farmer in Arizona, an impractical sort of man, given to hatching up lunatic schemes for amassing huge sums of money. Needless to say, they all ended in disaster and, to crown it all, they had four children, one of them mentally handicapped. Shall I continue, or does this bore you?'

'No, do go on!'

'A year or two before I went to visit Martha Teddy had begun to complain of not feeling well and he was also becoming clumsy and unco-ordinated in his movements, suddenly losing the use of his legs and so on. It worried them both and she persuaded him to see a doctor. The verdict was worse than anything they had dreamt of. He was suffering from an incurable disease and, even with drugs to alleviate it, his condition could only deteriorate. It would be a slow process, however, with no early release in death. He might live for another fifteen or twenty years, but long before that he would have become a helpless wreck, in need of round-the-clock nursing. It was a prospect that appalled them both and, to add to the bitterness, there was the knowledge that by the end of it their joint resources would be used up and there would not have been a penny left for the wretched daughter and her brood. What would you have advised them to do in those circumstances?'

'God knows. Pray for a miracle, I suppose; or the courage to take an overdose. I only hope I'm never faced with it.'

'They didn't believe in miracles and an overdose would hardly have solved anything. Insurance companies don't pay out for suicides. So what did that leave?'

There was a note of urgency creeping into Myrtle's questions now and I gave some thought to this one before replying:

'One way, I suppose, would have been to cook up a suicide to make it look like an accident.'

She rewarded me with one of her sweet smiles and nodded approval:

'What a clever girl you are, Tessa! That is exactly what I had hoped you would say.'

'Is that what they did?'

'Yes. To put it briefly, it happened one black and windy night by the East River in New York. It involved the ostensible suicide, or attempted suicide of a woman, whose identity was never discovered, either because she swam to safety, or because she drowned before her rescuer could reach her. However, there was a witness, another woman, who saw and was able to give a full account of the incident.'

'In the person of Martha, presumably?'

'How quick you are, my dear. Her testimony was graphic and entirely convincing, including her fruitless attempts to prevent Teddy from diving in, mainly because of his own weak health, of course.'

'And he really was drowned?'

'Oh yes, nothing spurious about that.'

'How terrible! But at least they achieved their object, so to that extent I suppose it could be called a success story?'

'No, it couldn't. Martha, so they tell me, is now a poor, lonely ghost, missing her beloved companion every hour of the day and haunted by the belief that if only they had put their faith in a miracle, none of it might have been necessary.'

'But at least the daughter is better off?'

'On the contrary. She has gained nothing and lost her monthly allowance as well. Knowing Martha, I'm sure she does what she can to help, but it wouldn't be enough.'

'Forgive me, Myrtle, but I was under the impression they had got away with it?'

'Oh yes, so far as that part of the plan went, there was no hitch. Everyone believed that Teddy was dead and, officially at any rate, that his death had been an accident. But there was one contingency which they had not foreseen. Under United States law no death certificate can be issued without a corpse to go with it. For legal purposes, eight years must elapse before a missing person can be presumed dead and Teddy's body was never found. It may still be buried under the mud and pollution at the bottom of the river, or it may have been swept out to sea. No one is ever likely to know and, if they did, it wouldn't help much now. The feckless son-in-law finally hanged himself, just to tie it all up for you.'

'No,' I admitted, 'that doesn't leave much in the way of silver linings and it must have been a nightmare for you, having known them both, but I still wonder why it knocked you out so badly that you can't write any more. Or, for that matter, where the witch-craft comes in?'

'Oh, come on, Tessa, you've been so good

up to now! You must try harder than that. I'll give you an outsize clue to get you started. Martha and I are no longer on speaking terms.'

'Sorry, that still doesn't help. I can't see how she would have fallen out with you over . . . unless of course . . . Oh, hang on a minute! It couldn't be that you'd already used the story in your book?'

'Bravo! That'll do nicely. And I'm grateful to you for assuming that it was written before and not after the event. Martha, unfortunately, didn't have such a high opinion of me.'

'Don't tell me she believed you capable of turning her story into fiction? If so, it can only be because she was temporarily so distraught. She must have realised by now how mistaken she was. Anyway, you told me the book was already with the printers by the time you were in America, so apart from anything else, how could there have been time?'

'It's obvious that you don't understand any more about the mechanics of printing and publishing than Martha did. It can take months, up to a year sometimes, before the finished work gets into the bookshops. The minute I got home I telephoned my editor to ask if she could possibly hold things up for a few weeks, so that I could make some alterations and revisions. I was too late, though. The wheels had already started to grind and pulling out at that stage would have involved untold complications and expense. Barring the threat of libel action, which was the least of my worries, there was nothing I could do to stop it.'

'But at that point couldn't you have warned Martha and explained how it had come about?'

'I should have, I know, but it's difficult to write such things in a letter. You really need to be able to watch the expression on your correspondent's face and gauge her reactions as you go along. Besides, I'm a moral coward and I kept putting it off. I told myself that I had eight or nine months' grace before the crunch and that the right opportunity to straighten it out was bound to come before that. At the very least, I might be able to tone down some of the more glaring similarities during the proof stage. It didn't work out like that though, and when the book was published in New York almost a year later I had a letter from

Martha, saying that she had bought a copy and was looking forward to reading it. It was the last I heard from her on that or any other subject.'

'How rotten for you!'

'Yes, it was. A bitter blow and not made easier to bear by the knowledge that I was in no way to blame. Unfortunately, too, it was only the first disaster of that nature, which culminated in my deciding that I had no option but to give up writing altogether. That has been the worst deprivation of all, I might tell you; worse, in a way, than losing an old and valued friend.'

'You mean something of the kind has happened again and that's what makes you believe you're a witch?'

'Exactly!'

'How very curious!'

'I guessed you might think so. The first one, naturally, I put down to sheer, maddening coincidence and soon after I got back from America I started work on a new novel. It opened with a man being arrested on suspicion of murdering his wife. He was a doctor in a small country practice and the rest of the story, right up to the last chapter, was told in flashback. It was really going along well and I felt chuffed about it. One evening when Jim, my rapscallion of a godson came to dinner, I really let myself go. He writes novels too, but his are in quite a different category, so there's no rivalry, but one can discuss plots and technicalities with him in a way which would be hideously boring and meaningless to any non-writer.'

'And what was his reaction?'

'He warned me off.'

'Oh, really. Why was that?'

'He was tactful about it, but I had the impression that he thought I was getting senile. He told me that only a few months earlier there had been a real life case which had followed almost exactly the pattern I had so painstakingly worked out. The chief suspect, who had also been a GP in a country practice, had been held in custody for several days, but eventually released. Jim said a lot of people still believed him to be guilty. I reminded him that all this must have taken place while I was out of the country and hadn't set eyes on an English newspaper for several weeks, and he agreed that this must be the explanation and that it was just an extraordinary coincidence. All the same, I could tell that he didn't really believe it and it was more likely that the poor old godmother's brain was getting a bit addled. And who shall blame him? Anyway, it quite took the heart out of me and I never touched the manuscript again. It's still around somewhere. I couldn't bring myself to chuck out something I'd toiled over for months. And perhaps one day I might go back to it again. I doubt it, though. Apart from everything else, I suppose it really could land me in a libel suit.'

'And did something of the sort happen again, after that?'

'Once more, yes. I'd only just got started on that one when the news broke. To tell you the truth, I hadn't worked out the details, so I don't know how close my story would have turned out to be to the real one, but there were enough similarities to convince me that I'd been cursed with some frightening sort of clairvoyance and that the only solution was to give up writing altogether. You may find that melodramatic, but it seemed like cold common sense to me.'

'Did you tell anyone about it?'

'Only Willie. In fact he saw what I had

written and I suppose he may have mentioned it to others. That's one of the things that bothers me and why I'm so hell bent on finding out what became of the manuscript I sent him.'

'What did he say when you told him?'

'To stop being a bloody fool. I had probably exaggerated the similarities between fact and fiction, or imagined some which didn't exist. On the other hand, if I had been given this extraordinary power of foretelling the future, well, so much the better. Properly handled, it could make very good publicity. He was very shrewd about things like that, you know, or thought he was.'

'And did you take his advice?'

'Yes, I always took his advice and I wanted to believe he was right. I decided to have one last fling and something he had said in that conversation gave me just the starting point I needed. The plot would hinge on an up and coming young public relations man, who sailed rather nearer the wind in exploiting the private lives of his clients than some of them cared for.'

'Until one of them murdered him, to shut him up.'

'Well, that's putting it rather baldly and,

naturally, there was a whole bagful of complications and red herrings dragged in to confuse the issue. I'd also got a sub-plot going, built around his wife. Near the end there's a whole chapter of dialogue between her and another man, a colleague of her husband's, when the two parallel themes come together and begin to overlap. It really comes off, I think, really stands out on its own and that's the rub. I'd hate to pare it down, but I was afraid he'd say that, as it stood, it upset the balance. Still, I mustn't prattle on about these silly little personal worries. Things have been getting bottled up inside me, that's the trouble, and I'm worse than ever without Willie to keep me in check.'

'But why, even if you do get this manuscript back, do you not intend to carry on with it?'

'Now then, Tessa, I've had to scold you about this before! You're not even trying. Obviously, nothing had happened in real life to duplicate my script by the time I sent it to him, otherwise I'd have torn it up, but how about what happened afterwards? I'll give you two seconds to work it out.'

It was as much as I needed, for one answer had already occurred to me. I considered it would be more delicate, however, for her to be the one to express it aloud, which she now appeared to have done.

3

The following day, exactly one week after the Alibi Club dinner, was the occasion for another luncheon à deux, although this one took place in a restaurant and was not pre-arranged.

My agent had been talking about the script of a television play by some female I had never heard of, which was provisionally scheduled to go into production in three to four weeks' time and which she considered would provide me with the very job to fill this unwelcome gap in my working life. The reason behind this thinking was that it was what she described as a short/short, the equivalent of a curtain raiser in the theatre, with only two parts, a man and a woman. Furthermore, since it was virtually in the form of unbroken dialogue, with only one set and no location work, the schedule would be limited to one week's rehearsal and three days' shooting. So it would be unlikely to conflict with such long term offers for my services as she felt confident would soon be flooding in.

Nor was I to get the misguided idea that these stringent conditions threatened anything in the way of a third rate, cheeseparing production. On the contrary, the director, who was under contract and therefore unaffected by the limitations of the budget, had stipulated that a high proportion of it should be spent on hiring the two best players available. This was flattering enough to break down most reservations and when I discovered that his name was Eric Ingles I was even able to stop asking myself how many others had turned it down before they approached me. This was because I had previously worked with him on two major productions, the second being the Willie Montgomerie play and, having good reason to believe that my liking and admiration for him was reciprocated, I felt confident that my name had been near, if not right at the top of his list.

So when my agent telephoned at midday on Thursday, to say that Eric was in her office, where they had been discussing terms and suchlike brass tacks and to suggest that I should join them forthwith for a preliminary script conference, I managed to keep a complaining note out of my voice when I reminded her that I had not yet been given the opportunity to read it. 'Eric knows that, my darling, and not to worry. You can do it when you get here. It won't take more than twenty minutes and you can raise any points that spring to mind, as you go along. You know how he likes to have that hand firmly on the steering wheel right from the start?'

I did know, and on the whole approved, so told her to expect me in half an hour.

It took longer to read than she had anticipated and I raised no queries as I went along. This was neither from want of concentration, nor because none sprang to mind. In fact, they were springing up like daisies in June, but they were the wrong questions and, after only one page, I knew I was reading it from the wrong standpoint; not hearing the characters' voices and picturing each scene in my mind, but wondering who the hell was the author of this play and how it had come into Eric Ingles' hands.

When I had read to the end I placed it

back on the desk and he said:

'Don't tell me! You're not happy with it, I can see that.' And then to my agent: 'She doesn't like it.'

'Yes, she does, my darling, she's ecstatic. I know that faraway, gormless look. She is trying to find the right words to tell you how marvellous it is.'

'Half right,' I told her, 'I am trying to find the right words to tell you that I do think it's marvellous and I don't think I can do it.'

'Good God, Tessa, it's made for you! What are you talking about? You could do it on your head.'

I felt like saying: 'But not with my heart,' but, realising that this would sound idiotic and pretentious, compromised with: 'It's nice of you to say so, Eric, and I'd love to believe you, but I still don't feel I'd be right for it.'

'Not enough comedy, you mean?'

'No, not that. I find it difficult to explain.'

'Tell you what, my angel. Why not take it home and have another little read? Then, if you're still doubtful you can show it to Robin. You always listen to him and he's bound to like it, he's so clever. Isn't that the most sensible idea, Eric?'

'No, it isn't. I'd like to get this mental block, or whatever, ironed out here and now. Why don't we go round the corner and have lunch at Martino's?'

'Yes, clever thinking, my darling,' my agent agreed, well up to her usual form in the role of one-woman arbitration and conciliation board, 'No good trying to discuss it on an empty stomach and the service is terribly slow, so you'll be able to iron it out at your leisure. Then you can come back here afterwards and report.'

'Aren't you joining us?'

'No, I've got a call coming through from New York at two o'clock. I shall be with you in spirit, though, and I just know everything's going to turn out fine.'

'Let's go then, Tessa, if you're agreeable?'

'I shall try to be,' I assured him.

Looking at his watch, after he had handed back the menu, Eric said: 'You have one hour to explain what this is all about, so start now!'

'And make it good?'

'No, I'd rather you didn't. Make it as bad as you like. What I'm hoping for is some fatuous objection, like you don't feel you're up to the weight, or it's outside your usual range and what will the fans have to say about that? If you feel there's something inherently wrong or false about the script, it's going to be a lot tougher to talk you out of it. I'm not sure I'd even bother to try.'

'What could it matter, so long as you believe in it yourself?'

'Which I do, but I could be wrong, couldn't I? I have deep faith in your judgement and I must tell you that a thumbs down from you would be a real confidence shaker.'

In my experience, this admission was far from typical of directors in general, still less those with the reputation and experience to match Eric's. Nevertheless, I believed it to be sincere. Outwardly so sure of his own superior judgement as to appear pig-headed on occasions, he was at heart a quivering jelly, fully conscious of his own limitations, of the gaps in his education and the many facets of life in which he had been at most a spectator and never a participant.

So I said: 'You can forget that idea. In

my opinion, there's nothing whatever wrong with the script. It's original and well constructed, full of subtleties and neat twists. I've only read it once, as you know, but I can assure you that my reservations have nothing to do with its quality.'

'Then what the hell are we arguing about? What else could . . . Oh, damn!'

My agent had been wrong for once in her life and our first course had arrived within five minutes. After that there was the wine to be inspected, tasted and felt for temperature, all of which was accompanied by rather more carry-on than it really warranted, signifying that this was another area in which Eric did not feel on very safe ground. I was grateful for the delay, though, for it gave me a respite in which to consider how many of my cards should be put on the table and how best to lay them out. When peace returned I said:

'If you really want the truth, what worries me is the author's identity.'

'What? What the hell are you on about now? How could that concern you?'

'*Loopholes* by Wilma Mathieson,' I said, leaning forward and reading from the label on the brown folder, which I had placed on the table beside my glass, 'It sounds false, somehow. Is it a pseudonym?'

'Could be, I suppose. To repeat: how could it matter?'

'You mean you really don't know who she is, or anything about her?'

'No . . . that is . . . No, I don't.'

'Did it come through an agent?'

'Not exactly, no.'

'So you're telling me that it alighted on your desk, out of the blue and with no introduction, whereupon you tossed everything else aside and read it, even though the author's name meant nothing to you?'

'Well, no, it wasn't as simple as that, naturally. It was passed on to me by someone whose judgement I had every reason to trust. So of course it took priority. Nothing unethical about that, is there?'

'Nothing, but you see Eric, unless I'm much mistaken, what you have on your hands with this one is a slight case of plagiarism.'

He did not, as I had half hoped, collapse into gales of laughter, or advise me to jump off a cliff. His dedicated and somewhat humourless approach to everything connected with his work forbade such levity and he said thoughtfully:

'I can see how you might have got hold of that idea. It is a curiously mature piece of work for a novice writer. Also, as you probably noticed, it's practically a final shooting script, as it stands, which argues a fair degree of technical experience in the medium. One explanation could be that Wilma Mathieson had some guidance in that area. Another, and to my mind, more obvious one, is that she has worked in some other capacity in television, assistant floor manager, or continuity maybe, and has learnt the ropes as she went along.'

'Unfortunately, there is a third possibility.'

'Several, I daresay. What's yours?'

'My theory hinges on the identity of this intermediary, whose judgement you rate so highly that you accepted his word and decided to push ahead, without asking any questions.'

'Then you can relax. It wasn't only his professional judgement I was talking about. He is, was rather, a man of absolute integrity.'

'Name of William Montgomerie, by any chance?'

'Funny you should ask that,' Eric replied, after a longish pause and not sounding amused. 'You're on the right lines. How did you guess?'

'The initials, for one thing. W.M. Also he did once tell me that he was keen to get a whole foot in television, after that dip of the toe. I thought he might have used this Wilma Mathieson stunt as a face saver, in case you told him the script was no good.'

'Even so, it was a fantastic guess. I suppose your dalliance in the world of crime and amateur detection has given you a flair for that sort of thing?'

'But you only said I was on the right lines. What did that mean?'

'It wasn't actually Willie who sent it to me. It only turned up a few weeks ago and he's been dead, as you know, since January.'

'Who, then?'

'His wife.'

'Oh yes, of course! Gwen!'

'You know her?'

'I know of her existence, naturally, but that's about all. I've never met her.'

'Nor me, but I had a letter from her about a month ago. The envelope was marked Personal and she'd put her name and address on the back. She said she'd come across this script when she was sorting out Willie's papers and she thought I might be interested, seeing as how I'd worked with him on the previous one and what a terrific admiration he had for me, and so on and so forth.'

'So you told her to go ahead and send it, which she did, and when you'd read it you rang her up and said it had great possibilities, or whatever phrase you use at that stage of the game. Then what? Did she tell you that Willie had written it himself?'

'Not in so many words, but that's obviously what she believed. For one thing, she'd made the Willie-Wilma connection, just as you did. For another, it was in very rough form, a lot of typing errors and so on. Presumably he'd been working on it when he was taken ill.'

'But it was properly typed when it got to you?'

'Oh yes. She said she'd got his secretary to do that.'

'In which case, she could have told at a glance whether it was typed on the same machine as the original?'

'That's right. And, no doubt, if it hadn't been, she'd have made a few enquiries about the authorship before contacting me. Personally, I feel entirely happy about it, but you know what your trouble is, don't you, Tessa? You've let this amateur detective lark get a hold on you. Talk about Reds under the bed! You've got crooks on the brain.'

'Yes, funnily enough, Robin was saying something like that only the other day. I didn't take it seriously.'

'I would, if I were you. I mean, why the hell, when you get right down to it, would Gwen want to pinch someone else's work and pretend it was her husband's? His reputation is doing all right without any boosting of that kind and it's not likely he's left her so hard up that she finds it necessary to turn a dishonest penny to make ends meet. I think you should be more careful about throwing these accusations around.'

'I haven't accused her of anything, Eric. It may have been a genuine misunderstanding on her part, or she may have been misled by Willie. All I'm saying is that I have a feeling he didn't write the original all by himself.'

55

'Yes, I gathered that, but you haven't explained why.'

'I can't tell you just now; not until I've cleared it with someone else. I'd like to hang on to the script for a day or two, if you don't mind, but in the meantime, without wishing to be alarmist, my advice is to call a halt until one of us has found out a bit more about Wilma Mathieson.'

4

'Will you invite her back?' Robin asked, when I had related the main points of interest arising from these two events.

'Who, Myrtle? Sure, why not?'

'And will you tell her about Eric's script?'

'I haven't decided yet. It needs thinking about.'

'Unlike you to be cautious.'

'I know, but you and Eric, between you, have undermined my confidence. Perhaps I really am beginning to see sinister motives where none exist. That's why I haven't mentioned this before.'

'Mentioned what before?'

'When I left her yesterday Myrtle threw out a not too heavily veiled hint that her chief anxiety about what had become of her script was that it contained an accurate forecast of Willie's death. In view of what she had told me about other examples of her clairvoyance and so on, I could understand how she would worry about it.'

'And now you're beginning to wonder whether you read a lot more into her parting remark than she intended? In other words, that she hadn't hinted anything of the kind?'

'No, I'm not. I haven't sunk so low in my own estimation as to believe I need things to be spelt out for me for their meaning to sink in. I'm quite sure that's what she meant to convey, but what I do begin to wonder is whether she was being quite so ingenuous as I had supposed. Perhaps, after all, she's in the same league as you and Eric and sees me as some nasty little busybody, who pads around sniffing out facts which decent people would prefer to ignore.'

'What if she does? You're not obliged to gratify her by living up to it.'

'Well, that's the real problem, you see. Does she honestly believe there was something fishy about it? If so, I don't mind having a shot at finding out what became of her manuscript, particularly as Eric has now been drawn into the game. On the other hand, I don't fancy being used in that way for some ulterior motive which she hasn't told me about.'

'Such as what?'

'God knows, but something of that nature happened to me once before, Robin, if you remember? Somebody once appealed to me to find out who in her family was trying to kill her. I fell for it and it turned out that my real job was to set things up in advance in such a way that when somebody was murdered I should be in a position to step forward and prove that the wrong person had been killed by mistake. I wouldn't want a repetition of that.'

'And so perhaps the first thing you should be asking yourself is whether the tale about forecasting events in fiction before they occurred in life was true, or whether she invented it to grab your interest?'

'You're right and that's a tough one too, isn't it? I'm strongly inclined to believe in the first disaster, the suicide that went wrong. All the same, I'm bound to admit now that there's nothing so very extraordinary about her having used the situation in a novel. An unfortunate coincidence, of course, as things turned out, but after all variations on that theme must have cropped up in dozens of plots. For all we know,

Martha or Teddy may have got the idea from a book in the first place.'

'Although I gather she claimed there had been a whole set of similar coincidences following that?'

'Two. Well, three, if you include what is supposed to have been in the rough draft which is now missing. But again that might have been sheer coincidence, or she might have invented it, just to get me interested and on her side. On the other hand, Robin, it can't all have been lies, or even poetic licence. I recognised the situation and characters in that television script the minute I started to read it. The similarity between it and the scene she had described to me in her book was quite glaring.'

'Yes, but remembering who it came from, she could have read it before you had lunch with her.'

'Right again! I hadn't thought of that and it's just about the last straw, don't you think? If she was lying there, it probably means that her own unfinished typescript never existed. If it did, the chances are a million to one that it has now been destroyed. How could one ever be certain of anything?'

'No way at all, so perhaps your best bet would be to stand aside and let things run their course?'

'That's always your advice Robin, and this time I wish I could take it, I really do. It's not obstinacy on my part, but I don't feel I can simply turn this job down without some very good reason. Eric's desperately keen to do it and I don't blame him. Anyone in his right mind would grab the chance, but he's also desperately insecure when it comes to backing his own judgement. Unless I can find a plausible explanation, he'll be stuck with the sneaking belief that I have no faith in it. Don't ask me why that should matter to him, but . . . Why are you staring at me with that glazed expression?'

'Because you've reminded me of something. Mrs Cheeseman left a message for you on the hall pad. Did you see it?'

'No, what does it say?'

'That a Mr Wiggle, or it could be Wiggly, rang and wants you to call him back. No number, so presumably he thinks you know it.'

'Then he was mistaken. I don't know anyone called Wiggly, or even Wiggle, do I?'

'No, but your mention of Eric has brought a ray of light. When you remember Mrs Cheeseman's track record, this practically rates as first past the post.'

'Ingles, in fact? It's worth a try,' I said, picking up the extension.

'You're showing off,' Robin complained, watching me dial, 'you can't really remember the number, just like that, without looking it up.'

'Yes, I can. To me they're like lines in a play. I can retain them for as long as they're needed and sometimes they come floating back, uninvited, after four or five years. Not that it's a trick worth slaving to acquire,' I added, putting the receiver back, 'because it only leads to foolish impulse. In the few minutes it would have taken to look up his number, I should have remembered that I still haven't the least idea what I'm going to say to him. As it is, he's not at home, so it comes to the same thing.'

'So why not start with Myrtle and see what reaction you get there? You might find that she's had second thoughts and would now like to forget everything she told you.'

'I can't see that as a very satisfactory solution to anything, but whatever you say,

Robin. Would you mind if I invited her to dinner on Sunday evening, when Toby will be here?'

'Not so long as you make it early, but haven't you got that wrong too? My understanding was that we'd been invited by your cousin Toby to spend the weekend with him at Roakes?'

'So we have and on Sunday afternoon he will drive back here with us and spend the night. The idea is to be as far away from home as possible on Monday morning, when there will be noise and confusion and furniture vans littering up the scene for miles around.'

'Why, is he moving out?'

'No, some new people are moving in; to one of the other houses on the Common, that is. He finds that sort of thing most unsettling, specially if there should turn out to be something unpleasant about them.'

'Why should there be?'

'Well, you know, dogs or children, for instance. He would prefer not to know about it until he has to. Any more questions?'

'No, quite clear now, thank you.'

'Then I shall busy myself with the telephone again and try my luck with Myrtle.'

Before I could do so, it tried its luck with me and, recognising the voice, I said:

'I thought I was supposed to call you?'

'You were, but I didn't have blind faith in your lady help to pass on the message and I didn't want to waste any time in telling you the news.'

'It's good, I gather?'

'Hopefully. We're in the clear.'

'Are we? How do you know?'

'Gwen, Mrs Montgomerie, has confessed all. You had me worried for a bit and when I got back to the office this afternoon I rang up and asked her straight out whether she knew for a fact and, if possible, could provide us with proof that Willie had written the script. I said our producer naturally wanted to use his name on the credit, but we wouldn't be able to do that if there was any risk of infringement of copyright and so forth.'

'And what did she say?'

'That we couldn't use his name because she'd written it herself.'

'Did she really? Well, I never!'

'With a little help from Willie, as she admits, although she claims the idea was entirely her own and all he did was offer a few suggestions here and there about tightening it up in the final stages. So no worry. Publicity-wise, it makes a good story and there won't be any legal tangles.'

'Why did she have to make such a secret of it?'

'Apparently, she was under the impression I wouldn't bother to read anything sent in by an unknown writer. So she started to try and overcome this problem by pretending that this Wilma Mathieson was a protégé of Willie's. When she saw that wasn't going to work, she switched over to letting me think he'd written it himself. That makes sense, doesn't it?'

'I suppose so.'

'You don't sound very happy about it. Is this the moment of truth?'

'How do you mean?'

'Well, dear, it's becoming increasingly clear to me that you were just throwing out that particular objection as an excuse. You weren't happy with the part and you didn't want to cut me to the quick by saying I was making a big mistake and it was a bloody rotten script. You may be right, but I wish you'd paid me the compliment of being honest about it, instead of treating me like a half-witted schoolboy.'

'That's not in the least how I'm treating you and I don't think it's a bloody rotten script, quite the reverse. All the same, Eric. . . .'

'Here we go!'

'No, listen. You remember there was a suggestion we should let Robin read it? Well, I'm in favour of that. Apart from anything else, there are one or two points concerning criminal law, which will have to be checked by an expert sooner or later.'

'Okay, ask him to read it, I don't mind. It could be helpful and it shouldn't take long.'

'No, but I don't want him to skim through it when his mind is already cluttered up with a lot of other business. I'd rather leave it till the weekend, if that's all right with you? Final decision not later than Monday morning.'

'Okay, I'm agreeable to that. Monday it shall be; and not later than ten o'clock.'

5

By the time we left Roakes Common on Sunday afternoon Robin and Toby had both read *Loopholes* and we were still dividing our conversation between this and Myrtle's excursions into the supernatural when we arrived back at Beacon Square an hour and a half later.

Robin had pronounced the script to be not half bad, a lot better than most, in fact, which, coming from him, was high praise although I suspected it was inspired mainly by the fact that Wilma had committed no howlers in her references to police procedure. More satisfactory still was that Toby, who is a playwright by profession and not always indiscriminate in his praise of other people's efforts in this line, was hard pressed to find anything irretrievably wrong with it.

His first words, when he and I met again at seven for the aperitif hour, were:

'Personally, I think you'd be a fool to let your scruples stand in the way. It's exactly what you need to make the bridge between this stereotyped light comedy character we've been seeing so much of during the past few years and something just a shade more profound and demanding. I shall despair of you if you don't grab the chance while it's going. They don't come often.'

'I realise that, Toby, and I agree, up to a point, but as I tried to explain to Eric, that's not the problem. Somehow, knowing, or at least strongly suspecting what I do, makes me feel uneasy about taking it on, without at least tipping Myrtle off about what's going on. Having confided in me, she surely has a right to believe that I'm on her side?'

'Oh, don't be so priggish! There are more important things at stake than her good opinion of you.'

'Priggish, if you say so, but practical too. She's bound to find out when the play goes out, if not before, and I have a feeling she won't take it lying down. It could land Eric and a lot of other people as well into one hell of a legal mess and I certainly don't want any part of that.'

'Not necessarily. As you've so often said

yourself, no one can doubt that the original manuscript has now been destroyed, if it ever existed. Since we are told that it was the only copy, Myrtle could never prove anything, however much noise she made. It would simply be passed off as the jealous ravings of a dead-beat author. Made all the more plausible, I should point out, by her own admission that she has failed to publish a single word for at least four years.'

'You may be right, Toby, and if you had said this to me three days ago you might have convinced me that it was a risk worth taking. Not any more, though. Now that Gwen has come bouncing out of her corner, all that has changed. So long as she stuck to her story that Willie was the author, I agree that she might well have got away with it. Now that she's committed herself to claiming the authorship, all that has changed. I daresay that with a good lawyer to act for her Myrtle would stand a chance. It might even occur to him to call me as a witness, if Myrtle tipped him off, and that wouldn't make a very good bridge in my career, would it?'

'I don't suppose it would do much harm.'

'Or much good either. Imagine having to

stand up in court and be teased or bullied into admitting that I had been aware all along that I was taking part in a conspiracy to defraud. And if Gwen were to get away with it can't you see how it could complicate the situation even further?'

'No, how would it do that?'

'By giving her the freedom to carry on with more of the same. It wasn't only this novel which Myrtle had given Willie to read, let me remind you. There are two more, both unpublished and both of which had been sent to Willie at some stage for his guidance and advice. Just think of the plunder waiting there for good old Gwen! I daresay she has enough material in her bottom drawer to last her for several years and by then she'll probably have gained enough experience, to say nothing of reputation, to get by on her own.'

'So you're determined to do the noble thing? Martyr yourself in the cause of truth and morality and blow her nasty, machinating schemes sky high?'

'It depends. I'll have to come down on one side or the other this evening because I've promised Eric to let him know tomorrow, but I suppose there's still a faint chance that I could be maligning Gwen. Everyone keeps telling me that I'm beginning to see villainy lurking round every corner, so perhaps it's true. I'm relying on Myrtle to come up with something to tip the scales one way or the other and I'm also relying on you, by the way.'

'A mistake, in my opinion. What for?'

'To back me up whenever you get the chance. And if you see the right opening before I do, for God's sake plunge in.'

'Then I had better have another drink. I always plunge more gracefully after the second. What time did you invite her for?'

'Seven to seven fifteen. I explained that we'd be dining early because Robin has a phobia about late nights on Sunday.'

'He may have to overcome it tonight. It is almost seven thirty now.'

'Oh dear, is it really? I do hope she's not going to be hours late, despite all my precautions.'

'All what precautions?'

'I asked if she'd like one of us to fetch her and she said there was no need because she could telephone for a taxi. They were frightfully reliable and always arrived on the dot.'

'Well, cheer up! She's probably had a heart attack and won't be coming, after all.'

'A fat lot of use that would be. At what point do you decide whether your dinner guest is sitting in a traffic block, or whether she has dropped down dead?'

At half past eight the decision was taken for us by Robin, who put an end to the discussion by going into the kitchen to heat up the soup.

During the interval I had twice rung Myrtle's number, each time getting the engaged signal, and had also suggested that we should go to her flat for an on-the-spot investigation, but there were no takers. Robin said that since she had settled down for a nice chat on the telephone, she had obviously forgotten her engagement with us, and that he had no intention of driving all the way to Swiss Cottage just to be proved right. Toby took an equally negative attitude.

At eight forty-five the telephone rang and a voice I did not recognise asked if that was Mrs Price.

I told her that it was and she said: 'You don't know me, but my name's Montgomerie, Gwen Montgomerie. I believe you . . . that is, you knew my late husband?'

'Yes, I did. Are you ringing about Myrtle, by any chance?'

'Well, yes, that's right, I am. How extraordinary! However did you guess?'

'Is something wrong with her?'

'Well, it's like this, you see. I'm afraid she's been taken ill. I didn't quite know what to do, to tell you the truth, but she'd told me she was having dinner with you tonight, so I thought perhaps I ought to give you a ring, otherwise you'd be worried. Well, I mean, anyone would.'

'Yes, I'm so glad you did. Is it serious?'

'I'm afraid so, yes. Actually, she's on her way to hospital. The ambulance left about ten minutes ago. The awful thing was that I couldn't remember who her own doctor was, so I rang up Dr Temple. He's . . . well, he's a friend and he knows about her case and luckily he was at home and able to come round right away and fix everything up. In fact, he's gone with her in the ambulance.'

'Which hospital?'

'Oh dear, I'm not sure . . . St something or other, I think it was. He did tell me the name, but it's all been such a shock. Would you like me to find out and let you know in the morning?'

'Yes, if you would. I'd be most grateful and thank you very much for telephoning.'

'Well, I thought I ought to let you know because you'd be expecting her. I daresay that was what brought this on. She always got so terribly over-excited about things and it was so bad for her. I rang her up about six o'clock, as I do most evenings, just to make sure she's all right and everything, but the number was engaged. So I thought to myself "Well, that's all right then. If she's talking on the telephone she must be all right," but I still couldn't put it out of my mind somehow, so about half past seven . . . .'

Five minutes later I replaced the receiver and turned to Robin.

'Myrtle's had a heart attack. That was Gwen and I'm afraid she has shown us up in a bad light.'

'I am growing accustomed to it,' Toby said, 'and I shan't allow it to worry me.'

'After she had tried the number and got the engaged signal for the third time, she tried to get the operator to find out if there was a fault on the line, but he kept her hanging on so long that she lost patience, hopped in a taxi and went to Myrtle's flat. To be fair, it wasn't nearly such a trek for her as it would have been for us. I remember Willie telling me that he lived somewhere near Regent's Park.'

'And what did Gwen find when she got there?'

'It probably took longer in the telling than the doing, but the gist of it was that she rang the bell and waited a couple of minutes, then opened the front door and went inside.'

'Really? Not locked?'

'She had the keys. She kept a set, as a precautionary measure against just such a emergency, after Myrtle had her last attack about a week ago.'

'And what did she find when she went in?'

'Myrtle unconscious on the bed, with the telephone receiver beside her. Presumably, she'd been trying to call for help, but passed out before she could dial the number. Anyway, Gwen managed to get hold of a doctor, who called an ambulance and off they went. Quite a simple story really, but it took her ages to get it out. She kept repeating herself.'

'Well, you wouldn't expect her to be very lucid in the circumstances. It's not an everyday experience to walk into a friend's flat and find her unconscious on the bed. Enough to fray the strongest nerves.'

'Except that she must have been prepared for something of the kind, otherwise she wouldn't have let herself in. And they weren't such dear friends as all that, you know. Myrtle was rather amused by the fact that someone she had always faintly despised should have set herself up as her guardian and protector. Gwen appears to have been inspired more by duty than affection. In fact, at one point she referred to Myrtle as though she was already dead.'

Toby laughed: 'I see it all now. This explains the cat and canary expression which has been so much in evidence for the past ten minutes. It struck me as a little out of place, in the circumstances, but obviously you believe, and not without cause, I admit, that having pinched Myrtle's story and publicly claimed it as her own, Gwen had no alternative but to hurry round to the flat and administer the fatal dose, which she has lost no time in doing. No wonder you smile!'

'You may be smiling too soon, though,'

Robin said. 'A simpler and more obvious explanation is that she realised as soon as she walked into the bedroom that Myrtle was already dead; or the doctor may have given it as his opinion that she was unlikely to recover. Either way, one wouldn't expect her to babble on about it to a complete stranger.'

'Oh, I agree with you entirely,' I said, 'and the smile is one of relief. At last I know what I am going to say to Eric tomorrow.'

'Oh, what is that?'

'To take a chance, if he wants to, but he must count me out. Talk about babbling on! One thing I am sure of is that the mind that conceived and worked out that well constructed, sharp and witty script could never have belonged to the garrulous lady I've just been listening to on the telephone.'

6

My agent was not amused and, never one to hide her feelings, went on about it at such length that I was eventually obliged to cut her short by explaining that I had to go to a funeral.

'Whatever for?'

'The usual reason.'

'Well, don't forget to wrap up warm.'

'Whatever for?'

'I've got enough trouble without you catching pneumonia. People are always catching pneumonia at funerals. It's a well known fact.'

'Not in June, surely? And let me assure you that this won't be some Gothic ritual in the Fen country, where we all stand around in the swirling mist, watching the coffin being lowered into the grave. It all takes place in some hygienic and cosy crematorium in North London.'

'Still, you can't be too careful. Who's dead? Anyone I know?'

'Shouldn't think so. A woman called Myrtle Sprygge. I don't suppose you've ever heard of her.'

'Oh yes, I have. I'm not so ignorant as you like to imagine. I met her once too, a couple of years ago. And we've still got a script of hers knocking about around here somewhere. I've been meaning to send it back for ages.'

'Too late now. Wasn't it any good?'

'Oh yes, not bad at all. Very good, as far as it went. It was the pilot for a six episode serial. Could have turned out a smash, but it was one of those deals that never got off the ground.'

'Did she send it to you out of the blue?'

'No, it was my partner's doing. He met her at some party and rather fell for those raddled charms. She told him about this idea she had for a television series and he knew Aurora Withers was looking for something on those lines, so he told her to bung it in.'

'But it didn't work out?'

'No, things looked promising for a time and then it all fell apart, the way they so often do. I forget what happened. Aurora lost interest, I expect, or decided she didn't want to be pinned down for ten weeks. I thought you were in a hurry to get to your funeral?'

'I am, but it always adds a touch of poignancy to the occasion if one knows a bit about the deceased during her lifetime.'

'Honestly, Tessa, this beats all! I've known you get up to some weird things in your time, but risking pneumonia for someone you didn't know sounds really morbid.'

'It is not so much for her sake,' I replied, 'as for the chance it may provide to meet one or two people who are still alive. And not only kicking, I suspect, but even now limbering up to dance on the grave.'

Aware of the rigid timetables which govern these conveyor belt obsequies, I took care to arrive only a minute or two after the appointed hour, so as to be in a position to observe the congregation from the back of the chapel when there was small danger of drawing their attention to myself. It was not more than two thirds full, and so offered plenty of choice, but there was an easily recognisable bare head in the centre of a pew with another occupant, about ten feet up from where I was standing. So I approached it from the side and installed myself at the end furthest from the centre aisle.

The owner of the head, who looked just as incongruous in a dark blue suit as he had in a dinner jacket, glared at me from under his bushy, russet eyebrows, as though I had committed some fearful gaffe. However, I did not waver, judging this to be his habitual reaction to anything which, by any stretch of the imagination, could be classed as unexpected. So it came as no surprise when, after the last rites were over, he dispensed with the formalities and barked out:

'Didn't expect to see you here!'

There must have been half a dozen possible answers to this, but unable to call one to mind, I responded with what I hoped would pass for an enigmatic, rather than inane, smile and, by means of a nod and a beck, directed his attention to the third occupant of our pew. She still remained huddled in her corner, even now that the principal mourners were drifting past her on their way out.

She was a thin, elderly woman, wearing flat heeled shoes, brown nylon raincoat and an outsize flat brown hat. This was as much as I could tell about her because she had kept her head lowered during the service, continually, as now, rummaging in her bag to take out a clean tissue and replace it with an overworked one. On the rare occasion when I had caught her looking up three quarters of her face had been hidden by the hat which was pulled down over it at a most unbecoming angle.

Realising, no doubt, that his only means of escape lay in dislodging one or other of us, the fox in the middle, best known, as I now recalled, as Nigel Banks, stretched his arm out to its full length and patted her awkwardly and a shade too vigorously on the shoulder. This so startled her that she jerked her head back and the hat fell over into the pew behind, revealing a long, thin, aquiline face, not without distinction, but greyish in colour and by no means so attractive that she could afford to saddle herself with such challenging headgear. In fact, her only visible charms were in her smile and the expression in her eyes which looked friendly, but at the same time vulnerable, as though she had gone through life steadily, obeying an instinct to like everybody on sight, in defiance of all the lessons it had taught her that her trust was misplaced.

'Oh, really now, Joyce!' Mr Banks protested, making a half-hearted attempt to retrieve the hat. 'Now look what you've done!'

'Oh, leave it, leave it, please!' she begged him. 'It's miles too big for me and I never want to see the beastly thing again. It was Gwen who insisted on my wearing it and I knew it was a mistake. Ought we to move on, do you think, before the next batch starts rolling up?'

She went ahead of us and when I had gathered up my bag and gloves and joined Mr Banks, who was tapping his foot in the aisle, I said:

'I hadn't realised you two knew each other.'

'Me and Joyce? Oh yes, known her for years.'

'And yet you were sitting so far apart from each other. Like strangers on a park bench.'

'Nothing personal. Trying to protect myself from her germs. Didn't you notice how she was streaming? Nose, eyes, all at it and hoarse as a raven when she opened her mouth. No business to be here at all, if you ask me.'

'I had put it down to emotion.'

'Don't you believe it! Tough as an old ox, Joyce. Got one of her head colds again, that's all it is.'

We had reached the door by this time and Joyce was hovering just beyond the threshold, evidently waiting for us. Two minutes in the fresh air appeared to have brought some relief to her condition, whatever its cause, although it turned out that Mr Banks' guess had been closer than mine.

'It's all right, really, Nigel,' she said defensively, 'I'm not infectious, it's only hay fever. Must have been all those wreaths that set me off.'

'Oh, bad luck!' he said, nevertheless keeping his distance. 'Have you met Theresa Crichton, by the way? Joyce Harman. Or is one supposed to say Mrs Robin Price?' he asked, switching some of his aggression to me, 'I never know where one stands in these matters.'

'In exactly the same spot as you do with a good many authors. Everything depends on the company you're in. You could simplify the problem by calling me Tessa.'

'It's Theresa Crichton, as far as I'm concerned,' Joyce said in her hesitant mumble, which gave the impression that she was talking to herself, 'I recognised you at once and I wanted to say . . . well . . . I was sorry to see about your last play. I thought it was jolly good. I saw a preview.'

'You were only just in time, unfortunately.'

'Yes, I . . . .'

'What I need is a drink,' Mr Banks remarked, jerking his head about, as though half expecting to see a waiter with a trolley mingling with the remaining groups of people scattered about on the grass outside the chapel.

'Turn left at the main road,' Joyce advised him. 'There's a pub called the Duke of something. It's not far.'

'The things you know, Joyce! Like me to buy you one?'

'Oh no, no, thank you, Nigel. I've promised to call on Gwen, you see, and it wouldn't do to keep her waiting.'

'No, course not. How about you . . . er . . . Tessa?'

'I'd love one, but I've got a date too.'

'Oh, shame! Raincheck then, perhaps?

Nice to have met you again. 'Bye, Joyce. Take care of that cold.'

'It's not a cold, it's hay fever. Oh, goodbye.'

'I wouldn't half mind a drink,' I told her, setting my feet in the direction of the car park, 'but it wasn't the most pressing of invitations. Can I give you a lift?'

'Oh, no thanks. I can get the bus.'

'Why do that when the car's here and I have to go that way in any case?'

'No, honestly, the bus goes almost to the door and I wouldn't want to put you to any trouble.'

'Why? Are you nervous of driving with strange females? Actresses, in particular, perhaps? I know the profession rates rather poorly with the insurance companies, but I'm quite safe, I promise you.'

'Oh, my goodness, no, nothing like that, I'm not in the least nervous. I don't drive myself, so if I were I'd never go in a car at all. It's just that . . . well, yes, I know I'm being silly. Thank you very much, I'd be most grateful for a lift.'

'It's true what you said,' I remarked, switching on the engine, 'the only people who never seem scared of being driven are the non-drivers. One thing I'm thankful for is not to have Mr Banks as a passenger. He'd probably have been a bag of nerves and it would have had the effect of sending me hurtling into the back of a bus.'

'Oh yes, poor Nigel, everything scares him. He's always like that, but he doesn't mean to be so ratty, you know. It's a form of shyness. I sympathise with that because I'm miserably shy myself. I expect that's why I'm talking so much. The trouble is that when we're together we bring out the worst in each other.'

'And is that why you wouldn't have a drink with him?'

'No, not exactly . . . well, yes, partly that, I suppose.'

'Yes, and of course, you have an appointment with Mrs Montgomerie, haven't you? What's her address, by the way? Somewhere in the Regent's Park direction, I seem to remember.'

'South Park Terrace. It's off the Marylebone Road. You turn left just past the High Street.'

By the time we reached Baker Street she had so far overcome her shyness as to have become silent and abstracted, staring out of the window like someone passing through a strange landscape. Then, coming back to reality, she said:

'It's the next one after this, but why not . . . I mean, you could drop me on the corner. It's a one-way street, so if you go down it you might find it difficult to get out again.'

'That's all right. I can't stop here without causing a major traffic jam, so I may as well go the whole way. Besides, having known Willie, I'm curious to see where he lived. What's the number?'

'Sixteen, but anywhere will do. Anywhere you can stop.'

'This looks like it,' I said, pulling up outside number sixteen, and Joyce went into another burst of shamefaced muttering:

'I wouldn't trust you not to wait outside until you've seen me safely into the house, so I'll have to own up. Gwen won't be there yet. She's gone to the hairdresser and I haven't brought my key.'

'Oh, good! So you and I have time for a drink, after all. Is there a decent pub anywhere near?'

'If you take the next turning on the right. It's a cul-de-sac and there's a place with tables out on the pavement. I think you can park there. A lot of people seem to.'

'Amazing!' I said, following her directions and finding them to be correct in every particular, 'Mr Banks was quite right; you really do know a lot.'

She was drumming her fingers on the table when I re-joined her on the pavement, not in an impatient way, but with deliberation, as though totting up her bills, or practising a scale. Catching sight of me, she withdrew her hand and slid it on to her lap.

'Sorry to be such an age, but the bar was rather crowded. Were you counting the minutes?'

'No, no, that's just one of my silly superstitions.'

'Finger tapping?'

'It's a sort of offering to the jealous gods.'

'You mean like touching wood thirty times?'

'No not exactly. It doesn't have to be wood. Paper is best.'

'How fascinating! Do tell me about it. I'm very interested in other people's superstitions, having some peculiar ones of my own. Does yours date from a long way back?'

'Oh, a long, long way back. Since my schooldays, in fact. It's awfully stupid and childish.'

'Tell me, all the same.'

'I was a rotten liar in those days, you see . . . still am, actually. I nearly always got found out and the favourite punishment at my boarding school was to write a hundred lines.'

'Like Bessie Bunter!'

'Except that I was so thin and tall, which was another misery. They used to call me beanpole. I got round shouldered from trying to look six inches shorter than I was.'

'What sort of lines were they?'

'Oh, awful! I had to write out a hundred times "Only fools and cowards tell lies". I'm not sure it's true, actually, but can you think of anything more stupid and tedious?'

'No, I can't. How does it fit in with the superstition?'

'One day when I'd transgressed again, and been hauled up for what I expected to be the usual ticking off from the head, was when it started. I was petrified of her and I got through the time while I was waiting to be admitted to the presence by tapping out that boring sentence and trying to set it to a sort of tune. When I got the summons to go in I found it wasn't going to be a wigging, after all. It was to tell me my mother had slipped on the ice and broken her ankle, and I was needed at home. Not that I was much use, but, well, you know, better than nothing I suppose and my mother didn't mind a bit about her ankle. She was a pretty, very indolent sort of woman, who really enjoyed spending all day lying on the sofa, so I didn't have to feel guilty about being glad it had happened, and I'm afraid that after that tapping out the tune became a habit.'

'And are the gods still keeping up the good work?'

'Most of the time, but it's more of a sinecure now. I don't tell nearly so many lies as I used to.'

'And maybe today's lapse hardly counted? I daresay you only invented the story about having to rush back to see Mrs Montgomerie out of consideration for Mr Banks' hypochondria?'

'Yes, but why did I have to go and pretend I had hay fever? That's where the penance comes in.'

'And, since you hadn't got a cold either,

presumably you were crying about Myrtle?'

'No reason to be ashamed of it, you'd have thought. But everyone else was so dry-eyed and unemotional I felt an utter fool.'

'If you ask me, that headmistress of yours has a lot to answer for. Was Myrtle a good friend of yours?'

'Oh yes, a good friend to everyone.'

'Did you meet her through Willie? I am right in thinking you were his secretary?'

'Yes, and now . . . well, I do a bit of work for Gwen. Just a few days a week. It's really more than she needs. Willie . . . well, he and I between us, I suppose . . . everything was in such good order there's nothing much left for her to do. Some people think creative writers live up in the clouds, but it wasn't like that with him . . . he had everything organised. But Gwen still insists on my going. It's because she feels lost and lonely, I expect. Her life revolved round Willie and now she has nowhere to go.'

'Why wasn't she at the funeral?'

'Out of respect to his memory, believe it or not. She was never allowed to go to funerals when he was alive. He didn't consider them suitable for women. I don't think I counted as a woman in that way, so

92

I could do as I liked, of course. I think Gwen felt badly about this one though, and that's why she made an appointment with the hairdresser. She's funny like that, she always flies to the hairdresser when life gets too much for her. It's her special kind of therapy. But she wanted me to be at the house by one o'clock, so that I could tell her about it and who was there.'

'He must have had a very strong character, and his influence didn't only extend to Gwen, apparently. Other women too seem to have depended on him for guidance and advice.'

'Oh yes, I suppose so. Who are you thinking of?'

'Myrtle, for one.'

'Oh yes, Myrtle. Yes, I suppose that's true, in a way.'

'She told me that she used to send him all her manuscripts for vetting, before she wrote the final version.'

'Well, yes, she did in the old days, but all that was over long ago. She hadn't written anything for years.'

'Are you sure of that?'

'Oh yes, quite sure. Willie often discussed it with me. She just seemed to run out of steam three or four years ago and gave it all up. I don't think it bothered her. She wasn't a dedicated writer like Willie. I can't imagine him ever losing the urge to keep on, however long he'd lived.'

'Curiously enough, that was rather my impression of Myrtle. Not that she wasn't a stayer, or had lost interest, but simply that her books had gone out of fashion and she'd become totally discouraged. You don't agree?'

Joyce brought her left hand out of hiding and looked at her watch. She then felt it necessary to justify this by explaining:

'I have to keep an eye on the time, otherwise Gwen will start fussing. She's a great worrier.'

'Well, it's only twenty to, so you don't have to rush. Was I wrong about Myrtle?'

'Oh, I couldn't swear to it and I mustn't speak ill of the dead, least of all such a good sort as she was, but I think most likely she was just trying to make it sound more interesting. She dramatised things a lot you know, and she'd much rather have seen herself as a tragic figure, a martyr to the fickle public, than someone who'd gone past her peak and grown bone idle in her old age.'

'As anyone would, I suppose, but it wasn't only her word. Willie told me, as well.'

I did not feel any compulsion to follow this statement with some finger drumming of my own, for I could no longer remember whether it was true or not.

'Oh, Willie! You shouldn't put too much reliance on anything he told you. He was always a bit soft where Myrtle was concerned. She could twist him round her little finger, as they used to say in my youth, and he would have thrown himself into any game she chose to invent.'

'Why was that, I wonder? Had they been in love at some point?'

'I suppose so . . . I mean . . . well, it's never happened to me, but I imagine that's the reason why most people get married.'

'Married? You don't mean she and Willie . . . ?'

'Didn't you know?'

'I knew he'd had another wife before this one, but surely it wasn't Myrtle? I'd have expected a name like that to stick in the mind.'

'It wasn't her real one. She was Mavis Spalding in those days, but when she wrote her first novel she thought Myrtle Sprygge would look jollier on the cover. It sort of caught on and most people have forgotten that it wasn't her real one.'

'Why did they divorce?'

'I suppose because he was . . . well, rather selfish and possessive. He encouraged her to take up writing and yet, somehow, when she made a go of it and became so successful, it didn't really suit him. Not that he was jealous, exactly, but it sort of made her independent of him. He wasn't any longer the be-all and end-all of her life. Gwen suited him much better in that way. She couldn't even buy herself a pair of shoes without his approval. It didn't stop him caring for Myrtle, though. I sometimes used to think they got on a lot better after they separated than before.'

'And how did Gwen feel about that? Didn't she resent this special relationship with the first wife?'

'Not as far as I know. If so, she never showed it,' Joyce said in a flat voice, at the same time scraping her chair to one side, so as to reach down for her bag, which appeared to have worked its way under the table. 'Which reminds me,' she added, having made quite a long business of retrieving it, 'I must be on my way, or she'll start worrying. Thank you for the drink and the lift. It's been a great . . . well, real treat meeting you and I'll look forward to seeing you in your next play.'

'If not before,' I assured her.

'She is like one of those maiden aunts in nineteenth-century novels,' I told Robin, who had opened the conversation by asking whether I had enjoyed the funeral, 'without trace of sophistication. What you might describe as sixty-five going on sixteen. Unfortunately, she is also extremely obstinate, with the obstinacy of an old woman and an adolescent rolled into one. She might drum her fingers on the table until they fell off, but she would never betray anything she did not wish me to know.'

'And I fail to see why you should want or expect her to. There could hardly be anything she would feel it necessary to conceal about Myrtle's death, if that's what you were after?'

'Oh, you checked on that for me, did you? Thank you, darling. Does it mean that she did die of heart failure?'

'Well, in a sense, I suppose everyone dies from that in the end. In this case, though, it was a chronic cardiac condition, which would have carried her off at any time, particularly of course if she'd had the misfortune to get an attack when she was on her own.'

'Could they tell how long she'd been in a coma when Gwen found her?'

'I have no idea. All you asked for were the bare facts, as they appear on the death certificate. Presumably, as it was Sunday evening, she could have been lying there for anything up to twenty-four hours. If this were a murder case, I daresay it would be possible to find out if anyone had seen or spoken to her on the telephone during Sunday afternoon, but it isn't and so it wouldn't be.'

'I know that Robin, and I never suggested anything of the kind. That was just Toby trying to be funny. How about Willie, though? Was his an equally natural death?'

'If not more so. He had a liver haemorrhage, was whipped off to hospital and died within two days.'

'So Myrtle's worry can only have been that she had described something just like that in the manuscript she'd sent him and, lo and behold, it all came true only a few months later. Well, that would be enough to alarm anyone and it's no wonder that her clairvoyance was beginning to unnerve her. My mistake was in carrying it a stage further and assuming that she was hinting there was something fishy about his death and that what she had actually described was a murder method which someone had then made use of. It was gilding the lily because she had enough to worry about without that complication, but I suppose you had all dinned it into me that I was looking for murderers under every stone and I was fooled into believing that Myrtle had hit on the same idea and was hoping to use it for her own ends.'

'And I daresay you are secretly a shade disappointed to discover that the idea had never entered her head?'

'Not at all, I am relieved. How often must I say it?'

'Not again, I promise you. I'll lay off now, although I'm afraid it does mean that life is going to be rather bleak for you, unless your agent comes up with something fairly nippily to save the day. Perhaps you should look for a new hobby to tide you over?'

'I don't need tiding over, thanks all the same, Robin, or a new hobby either. I start rehearsals next week.'

'Oh, congratulations! Why didn't you put me out of my misery before?'

'I only decided to accept it about two hours ago.'

'So tell me all about it.'

'You know about it already. It is Gwen Montgomerie's very own little masterpiece, with Eric Ingles directing.'

'What? You mean you've climbed down from your pinnacle of righteousness, and agreed to do it, after all? I can hardly believe it.'

'I changed my mind, you see.'

'Yes, obviously, but why? Did they talk you into it?'

'No, it was my own doing. It struck me, when I was driving home after my chat with Joyce, that I was never going to get anywhere with her, whatever tricks I used. I'd taken it as such a stroke of luck, meeting her like that and getting to know her a bit, but it wasn't going to work out and I'd have to play the hand another way. The fact that everyone who's read this play is so impressed by it naturally made it easier, but that wasn't the main reason for saying I'd do it. The other one carried even more weight.'

'Which other one? I don't follow you.'

'Well, you see, Robin, as you've pointed out, there are no crimes of violence to be considered here, but then, as I've said a good many times, I never seriously imagined there would be. On the other hand, the crime of plagiarism may still be very much with us. In fact, Myrtle's death has made that aspect more crucial than ever, since she's no longer around to fight her own battles.'

'Quite so, but I'd have expected that to make you more reluctant to aid and abet the conspiracy, not less. I rather saw your quixotic streak coming out with bangles and bells on it in this situation. Sacrificing your career in the cause of truth and justice and all that lark.'

'I hope it won't be sacrificed beyond repair, but you're absolutely right. That is what I had in mind.'

'Funny way to go about it, is all I can say. Eric has a far better chance of turning out a mini-masterpiece with you in his team and how could that fail to benefit the perfidious Gwen?'

'We'll see about that, but in the meantime you can't tilt at windmills by staying indoors and keeping the curtains drawn. So long as Myrtle was available, with her inside knowledge of the facts and the people concerned, we might have pulled it off between us, but I'd be lost on my own. I wouldn't know where to start and every door would be slammed in my face. This way I'll at least get both feet inside one of them.'

'Not very far inside, surely? I thought authors were kept firmly at bay, once their job was finished?'

'Not always. Much depends on the director and Eric is a great one for team work and everyone pulling together. Besides, from what I did manage to glean from Joyce, Gwen is bored silly and spinning round in circles, looking for ways to fill the empty hours. So she won't be able to resist the slightest encouragement to be drawn into the proceedings, and I shall be there to see that she gets it.'

7

Crispin Foreman had been cast for the role of Henry in *Loopholes,* a move for which I awarded Eric A plus marks. Cris, as he was known to his numerous friends and enemies, had been established as a major actor for at least fifteen years and had starred in any number of plays and films, both classic and modern. He had also been known to whip the honours from under the noses of children, dogs and capped teeth stars, playing two brief scenes in a minor role which most actors would have considered unworthy of their talent.

So it was an endorsement of Eric's professional standing that Cris should have been eager to take part in this comparatively lightweight production, but this was not his only triumph. The truth was that Crispin, both as an individual and a product of his background, represented everything that

Eric most deplored in the human race. He was the son of an eminent QC and an earl's daughter, had been educated at a famous public school and gone one better than his father by marrying the daughter of a duke. Furthermore, he had profited so little from these material advantages as to have acquired a reputation for being a conceited and arrogant snob and singularly lacking in humour. So it spoke well for Eric's artistic integrity that, in offering him the part, he had not allowed personal prejudice to interfere with professional acumen. He was also eager for assurances that I was happy about it.

'You mean resigned to being outclassed, acted off the screen and back into the small league where I belong?' I enquired and he gave me an affectionate pat:

'No, no, dear, no danger of that. Yours is by far the better part, longer too and it's tailor-made for you. That means you'll be evenly matched, which is what I was after. You're the reason why it was essential to get a really first rate actor for Henry. Otherwise, it would have thrown the balance and we'd never have been able to build up the tension.'

I was not altogether convinced by these soothing words, but, considering that I had given him a rough enough ride already, without piling on fresh burdens, I said:

'I shall look on it as a challenge.'

This being an acceptable word in his language, he nodded in solemn approval and the meeting concluded in a spirit of perfect harmony.

'Right! See you at nine o'clock on Monday for a read-through. Oh, and by the way, Tessa, I've invited Gwen to sit in at rehearsals. She's dead keen to do that and I think it's essential that we all keep in step from the word go. You don't mind?'

'No, Eric, why should I mind?'

'Just checking. Well, that's all right then, so long as you're happy about it.'

'Oh yes, thank you, very happy indeed!'

She had not arrived by the time we met in a converted pre-fab for the first rehearsal, but her absence scarcely impinged at the time, two thirds of my attention being focused on the spectacle of Crispin Foreman in full costume at nine o'clock on a Monday morning. It consisted of faded couture jeans, an expensive and split clean though well worn pink shirt, open necked and with a silk scarf tucked inside, and ankle length canvas boots. He looked like a fashion photographer's version of an assistant cameraman, which had no doubt been his intention, and his behaviour was ostentatiously subdued, in a matching style. This, we realised, was the modest, self-effacing Crispin, intent, like the good trouper he was, to come down to our level, cut out the frills and get on with the job in hand. It had the effect of making me feel both dowdy and over-dressed, but I could see Eric had accepted it all at face value and felt happy that things were getting off to a good start.

'What does that line mean, would you say?' Cris asked about one hour later, then repeated it, reading in a flat, monotonous voice:

'You had us all fooled there, didn't you, Myra? I daresay I was the only one who saw through the elaborate pretence?'

He then looked up and repeated the line, but slowly and with more emphasis. 'Sorry to be so thick, but I don't get it.'

'What's your problem?' Eric asked.

'For a start, it doesn't make sense. Not important perhaps, but hardly the sort of ponderous, inept remark one would have expected from Henry. He is supposed to be an educated man presumably, and either Myra had them all fooled, or she didn't? So if Henry had seen through her, surely it must follow that she didn't? Furthermore, why are we only given the information at this point? There has been no indication until now that Henry did see through her. Oughtn't there to be some hint of this earlier on? Forgive me if I'm wrong.'

'No, no, I take your point and hopefully we can soon get it ironed out. Perhaps I should have a word with Gwen. Has Mrs Montgomerie arrived yet?' Eric asked, raising his voice so that it would carry to the corner where the floor manager, Yvonne, and one or two of her cohorts were gathered together.

'Don't think so, Eric. I haven't seen her.'

'That's strange! It was fixed for her to be here by about nine thirty. Could she have got lost, do you suppose?'

'Yes, easily. Want me to go and make some enquiries and organise a search party?'

'Oh, would you, Yvonne? I'd really appreciate that. I did tell her exactly how to find her way here, but I've heard of people spending hours traipsing around, looking for this place, especially writers for some reason.'

The reading continued for another twenty minutes, at which point Yvonne re-entered the studio, giving the thumbs-down signal.

'No luck?'

'Sorry, no. She hasn't been seen or heard of. What next?'

'Not to worry, I'll give her a ring myself in a minute. Time for a break, anyway. Back here at two o'clock. Okay, everyone?'

I had an engagement to fulfil in the Wardrobe, where I ran into several friends and former colleagues, including our current costume designer. He was, as usual, bursting with scandalous information, related and unrelated to his craft, and it was nearly half past one before I could tear myself away and go up the canteen.

Cris was seated alone, wearing the vacant expression of an actor who is not being fawned on, so I carried my tray over to join him.

'Any news of the missing author?' I asked, when I had laid on what I considered to be the requisite amount of fawning. 'Has she turned up yet?'

'No. Eric telephoned her house, but was unable to speak to her.'

'You mean there was no answer?'

'No, I do not mean there was no answer. He spoke to her secretary, whose function at present appears to be fending off telephone callers.'

'Did she say so?'

'Not in those words. It seems that Mrs Montgomerie has been laid low by a severe attack of laryngitis. She is unable to speak above a whisper and has been advised by her doctor to stay at home and not answer the telephone until such time as it passes off. Eric is not altogether happy about it.'

'Didn't he believe her?'

'Who's to say, but I gather that, when asked for details about the likely duration of this embargo, the secretary became rather confused.'

'Oh, I see,' I said, picturing Joyce, with the telephone clutched in her right hand while the left one tapped out the familiar refrain. 'All of which leads Eric to suppose that she has changed her mind and the laryngitis is just an excuse to back out?'

'Which is quite a puzzle, isn't it? In my experience, most authors would jump up from their death bed for the chance to throw their weight about and preserve their immortal lines intact.'

'Not this one, according to Eric. Insecure was the word he used to describe her.'

'And they're usually the worst. However, I am willing to concede that there may be something about this lady, which sets her apart from her fellows. Frankly, my darling, I am puzzled.'

'Are you really, Cris. What has puzzled you?'

'I am wondering if there is a touch of the schizo in the make-up.'

'How interesting! Do go on!'

'It's such a curious mixture, don't you see? A first rate script, as I am sure you agree, otherwise you wouldn't be here at what Eric would doubtless call this moment in time. Furthermore, I find most of the lines quite exceptionally natural sounding and easy to get the tongue round. One would have said there was a lot of experience there of working with actors. Was she one herself, do you suppose?'

'I don't know, but that wouldn't have made her schizophrenic. Or would it?'

'I merely wondered whether this facility

for writing dialogue was instinctive and that when she brings her mind to bear on it and tries too hard she goes to pieces. Practically every line is so tight and pointed and yet every now and then you come to one which a child of ten would find unacceptable. It interests me. Not enormously though, and personally, I shall not complain if the laryngitis is with us for the next three weeks.'

'That wouldn't please Eric.'

'Oh, Eric would learn to live with it and I'm sure he'd be much better off without her. We all should. We'll be in a real pickle if she turns up with her six-year-old mind and leaves the instinctive one at home.'

'If it's any comfort to you,' I told him, 'I think that is the very hazard which may now have occurred to her. We had better try and work on it.'

In our pre-fab again for the afternoon sessions, the floor had been taped in geometrical patterns, as for a complicated game of hopscotch. Scripts in hand and taking care not to walk into a section marked SOFA or DESK, we went through our movements for the opening scene.

We were all set to embark on this exercise

for the second time when there was an interruption. Someone knocked on the door, then opened it a tentative inch or two and Yvonne went across and pulled it wider. Two scared looking women stood on the threshold and there could be little doubt that the younger was Gwen, the other being Joyce, who was also spokeswoman:

'Is it all right to come in? I mean . . . we shan't be in the way, or anything?'

'Not in the way at all. Delighted to see you! Do come in!' Eric said, moving to the door with a hesitancy which did not quite match his words. 'How are you, Gwen? Feeling better now?'

'I'm . . . er . . . afraid I have to do the talking,' Joyce said, not making a good job of it. 'Gwen wanted to come, but she's only been allowed to on condition that she doesn't use her voice. Unless it's absolutely necessary, I mean, if you see . . .'

'Oh yes, and you're . . . ?'

'Joyce Harman. I think we've . . . that is, I think we've spoken on the telephone. I don't know if you remember. I was Willie's secretary.'

'Yes, of course I remember. Well, let's see if we can rustle up a couple of chairs and put you over by that table there, with Alison. Alison is our continuity expert, by the way. You've got a script?'

'Yes, oh yes, we brought one with us.'

'Good, then I'll just show you where we've got up to and what we're doing and you'll be able to pick it up as we go along. And, if you have any queries, Gwen, just make a note of them and we'll hammer them out at the end of the session.'

Throughout this dialogue Gwen had been nervously mouthing and smiling her acknowledgements, which she continued to do, while Eric continued to fuss around her. She was small-boned, with a pale complexion and faded blonde hair, and was wearing a pale blue dress, which I felt sure the saleswoman had not omitted to point out perfectly matched her eyes. There was something doll-like about her, but it was a doll that had seen better days, and watching her as carefully as I was able to from that distance, it occurred to me that being so much younger than her husband and most of his friends she had become stuck with the idea that she was younger than everybody and would remain so forever.

Crispin, meanwhile, was competing for

my attention with some deliberately asinine questions about the practicality of growing gooseberries in a London garden. I took this as evidence that he had become seriously disturbed by this intrusion into our little coterie, since I was the last person to give advice on that subject, as I pointed out to him.

'Our garden consists of two window boxes, and a man with a van comes twice a year to change the plants over. If you're so mad about gooseberries, why not have them delivered from one of your castles, or inform Fortnum's of your requirements?'

'The point is that Charlotte thought a battalion of those spiky bushes might help to keep the marauding cats out.'

'Oh, I see.'

'So, having disposed of that, isn't it your turn now?'

'My turn for what?'

'You could ask me whether Charlotte has a phobia about cats, or whether I'd spent much time twiddling my thumbs in a television studio lately.'

'Yes, it is rather frustrating, I agree, but Eric has his methods and we must try to bear with him because they usually pay dividends.'

'Quite right my darling, and we shan't have to bear with them for very long, shall we? Quite a tight little schedule, all things considered, wouldn't you say?'

'Oh, indeed!'

'Oh, indeed, as you so neatly put it. We shall have our work cut out to get through at all, I shouldn't wonder. But of course the author must come first, I do see that. I hope I know my place by this time.'

He had succeeded in making it clear that he would have preferred his place to be anywhere but the one he was in and I stared across at the corner of the studio, willing Eric to come back and pay some attention to us before open rebellion broke out. The message must have got to him too, because at the same instant he turned round and walked towards us.

'Okay, everyone, all set now. Let's take it from the top of page four, shall we?'

The rehearsal continued for another hour and a half without further interruption and then we had a ten minute break. Eric said:

'I'll just go and put Gwen in the picture about those two or three points you raised,

Crispin. She might be able to iron them out for us here and now.'

'I hardly see there could be much to prevent her doing so,' Cris replied affably, 'since it requires no more than half a dozen new lines.'

'Oh, quite; but she's feeling unwell, as you probably saw. She may need a little time to sort it out.'

'And time, of course, is of the essence.'

'I'll see what can be done,' Eric said uncertainly, and evidently noticing for the first time that Crispin was not entirely happy.

Unfortunately for the safe passage of our ship, his forecast had been correct, as was conveyed to him by a combination of nods and shakes of the head, backed up by voice-over from Joyce. Gwen was not at present feeling quite up to the task required of her.

'So here's what we'll do,' our go-between explained, returning once more to base, 'She'll take the script home now and she and Miss Harman will work on it this evening. They'll let us have the new lines in time for tomorrow's rehearsal. That would seem to be in order.'

Crispin had not spent all those years in front of the cameras without his eyebrows learning a trick or two and no words could better have expressed his amusement than they did then.

'I think we should go along with that,' Eric said, thrown on to the defensive. 'It's important, in my view, to get everything right, down to the last detail, from the outset and it's a waste of time trying to communicate in the current situation.'

'Time of course being the last thing we can afford to waste,' Crispin agreed.

'Right, then!' Eric said, asserting his authority and not before time. 'So let's run through it once again, shall we? Starting from your first entrance. Okay, everyone?'

No conflicts arose during the remainder of the afternoon session. Eric had worked out every move in advance with exemplary precision, and with the interlopers no longer present to exacerbate him, Crispin's confidence returned. In the most literal sense of the term, he did not put a foot wrong from start to finish.

Sadly, though, this good behaviour did not bode any better than the tantrums which had preceded it. There was a briskness now in his manner, demonstrating all too clearly a purely businesslike attitude to the job, as one to be got through with the maximum speed and efficiency. There was no time for irrelevancies or jokey asides. Nor did the austerity relax when the rehearsal finished and we reverted to our true identities. Eric made the conventional gesture of inviting all present for a drink in the bar before we dispersed, but Cris excused himself by explaining, in the tone of one who cared not whether anyone believed him, that he and Charlotte were going to the opera and he had to be home early to change.

None of this held out much promise for the chummy, pulling together atmosphere, which was the one above all in which Eric thrived, and I felt no more happy about it than he did. Ironically enough, I could not fail to see that the single element in this undertaking that I had taken for granted would be flawless, namely the quality of the production, was now most in jeopardy. Obviously something had to be done to stop the rot before it could spread any further, and I spent the whole of the journey home, the remaining thirty minutes before Robin returned, and one or two of the small hours as well, pondering what form it should take.

8

Before leaving for the studio on Tuesday morning, I took the plunge and telephoned the house in South Park Terrace. As I had anticipated, it was Joyce who answered. She recognised my voice and I said:

'Sorry to call so early, but I may not get another chance. How's the patient?'

'Oh, well, I can't tell you really. She's still asleep, you see. At least, as far as I know, she is. Do you want me to find out?'

'No, don't bother with that. I was only wondering whether she'd been able to make those script changes yet?'

'Well no, I'm afraid not. She was feeling pretty bad by the time we got home, you see . . . raging headache and everything, but we're hoping to get started on them this morning. Perhaps . . . .'

'What?'

'Perhaps you could pass that on to Mr

Ingles for me, if it wouldn't be any trouble? Gwen said I was to ring him this morning, but I do so hate bothering people . . . men . . . when they're working. If you wouldn't mind just letting him know that she's hoping to get to work on it today, or tomorrow at the latest?'

'No, I'm awfully sorry, but I think it will have to come from you, Miss Harman. It's not strictly my business, although I do think that perhaps the time has come for you and me to have a private talk, if you could arrange it?'

'Oh dear, well, I really don't know if . . . . What about?'

'The script, mainly. Could you possibly meet me at that pub we went to before? Say about six thirty this evening?'

'I don't know. It would depend on Gwen, you see. She might not be well enough to be left on her own.'

'Surely she could manage for half an hour?'

'It's the telephone, you see, that's the trouble. If the telephone should ring she wouldn't be able to answer it and she'd be worried.'

'Take it off the hook when you leave and

they'll think the number's engaged and try again later. Look, I tell you what, Miss Harman, think it over and see what you can do. I'll be there, anyway, so if you're absolutely stuck you can leave a message at the bar.'

'Oh, but I wouldn't want you to . . . .'

'Sorry, I have to go now, or I'll be late for work.'

'How did the . . . er . . . rehearsal go?' she asked when I joined her at the pavement table, where I noticed that she had remembered what I had been drinking at our previous meeting.

'Not too bad, all things considered. By "all things" I refer, of course, to the fact that we didn't have the revised script to work on.'

'Yes, I apologise for that, but Gwen hasn't been feeling . . . .'

'Up to it? No, I guessed that, but cheer up! It wasn't an insuperable problem. Things didn't go very easily at first, but in the end we just cut out the ambiguous bits and stuck in a couple of words to join up the sequence. It worked quite well and I wonder Gwen didn't think of it herself.'

'I believe she thought something more inventive was needed.'

'And, of course, having destroyed the original script and not possessing that kind of inventiveness herself, she was a bit stuck?'

'I'm sorry, I don't quite follow you.'

'Yes, you do,' I said, watching her left hand, which was poised to go into action, 'and this doesn't call for any finger tapping. Nothing you could say would ever convince me that Gwen wrote that script alone and unaided, so however much you may protest that she did, you won't be deceiving anyone.'

Joyce raised her hand and gazed at it, as though it had let her down in some way. Then she said:

'How did you find out?'

'In a number of ways, but I suppose the laryngitis clinched it. Such a convenient complaint, from her point of view, enabling her to go about and live a relatively normal life, including visits to the hairdresser, I daresay, while quite unable to answer awkward questions. How about you? How long have you been in on the secret?'

'Almost from the beginning, I suppose.'

'Did you work it out for yourself, or did she tell you?'

'Oh Lord no, she never said a word and I didn't mention it either. She'd have been livid. It was really when I was typing it out for her that I began to be so puzzled. "Fancy Gwen," I thought to myself. "All these years we've been thinking of her as rather childish, well, almost illiterate you might say, and all the time there was this other character, a sort of instinctive writer, locked up inside her and waiting for the chance to come out." '

'What made you change your mind?'

'I suppose one thing just led to another. I had to query one or two clumsy phrases and repetitions as I went along, and she was always so vague about it, or else she stormed on about how I didn't know what I was talking about. Once she told me that if I thought I was so clever the best thing would be to re-write the passage myself and stop bothering her. Well, you know, that didn't sound like most authors I've known and that's when I began to wonder whether it really was her alter ego that had written it, or whether someone else had.'

'And perhaps you had also recognised

something in the form and style of the dialogue which gave you a clue as to who that someone else might have been?'

'No, I can't say I had, I'm not clever enough for that, but in any case there couldn't be any doubt about who it was.'

'Who?'

'Well, Willie, surely? It must have been some manuscript she came across when she was turning out his papers, an idea he'd had for a television script and then dropped. Naturally, she would have been tempted to use it to earn some money. One can sympathise with that.'

'Yes, but why sail under false colours? Why steal the honour and glory as well? She'd have got the fee and royalties anyway.'

'Oh no, she wouldn't. That's the big snag and why I was on her side and tried to help her all I could. It's also why I can't help feeling sorry that you should have . . . well . . . not interfered, because that would sound rude . . . but caught her out. It was quite a harmless little deception, wasn't it, given the circumstances?'

'What circumstances?'

'Well, you see, Miss Crichton, unlike

what a lot of people believe, Willie didn't really have all that much to leave. He didn't own the house, you know. It's only on lease, which runs out in about two years, so that's not much use and he spent practically every penny he earned. He was very generous, for one thing, but that's not going to do poor Gwen much good. She has practically no capital and she's got used to living this kind of life, so it's going to be hard for her to come down to the poverty level again. All she has is her widow's pension and the royalties from Willie's books and they're bound to dwindle as the years go by, aren't they?'

'I suppose so but you still haven't explained what advantage there is in putting her own name on this script instead of his. The money would be paid to her in any case.'

Joyce shook her head: 'Well, no, it wouldn't, you see, Miss Crichton. I'm afraid I'm awfully bad at explaining things, but that only applies to published work, which he'd been paid for already, so to speak. All the unpublished stuff, from rough jottings right through to completed short stories, was left unconditionally to this American university, who have the archives for the

Montgomerie Collection, as they call it. It was a silly arrangement really and I can only think that he never imagined himself as dying. Anyway, I'm sure he believed he had years and years ahead of him and all the time in the world to make provision for Gwen. But as things stand, legally speaking, this script is the property of the university and she wouldn't be entitled to a penny, if it ever came out that he'd written it.'

'Oh, I see! Well, yes, that would be an incentive for a little fiddling, I must admit.'

'So I do hope you won't give her away? After all, it can't do any harm, can it? Nobody stands to lose anything except the university and I don't suppose they're short of money.'

'No, indeed, but there still remains one tiny snag, which hasn't so much to do with money. It's more a question of reputation. At least, I think it is, although there could be any amount of heirs and beneficiaries who are going to be done out of their dues, for all I know.'

'I'm sorry, you must forgive me, Miss Crichton, but I'm so slow and I don't really understand you. I thought I'd explained how Willie disposed of everything? No one, apart from Gwen, has any claim on it at all.'

'Yes, you have, but the point is, are you absolutely sure that this particular script, along with others which may come to light in the future, actually was his property to dispose of?'

'Well, yes, of course . . . I mean, who else's could it have been?'

'I don't know, but I thought, as his secretary, who saw all his correspondence and worked so closely with him, you might have some ideas of your own about that?'

'Me? No, certainly not, nothing of the kind. It would have been quite impossible for anyone but Willie to have written it. I'd stake my life on that.'

It was a valiant try, but it would have been a lot more successful if it had occurred to her to ask the obvious question, which was whether I had any suspicions of my own about the true authorship. Better still, perhaps, if she had been able to resist sliding her left hand under the table.

'Nevertheless,' Robin said, 'you have decided not to pursue it? You will not be letting any cats out of this bag?'

'No, I've dropped my private crusade to

ensure that credit went where credit was due, for the time being, at any rate. It is too late to pull out and my duty now is to the living and, in particular, Eric's happiness, on which so much depends.'

'How about Crispin, though. Won't he continue to raise hell until he gets the script tidied up as he wants? How are those two poor floundering ladies to cope with that problem?'

'They won't have to, if they follow my advice. I suggested to Joyce that, between them, they should compose a letter to Eric, to get Gwen off the hook. She must explain that she was more seriously ill than had been realised and had been ordered by her doctor to lay off work for several weeks. Furthermore, her brief excursion into the intricacies of television production had taught her that she lacked experience for the job which was now required of her and considered that some professional script writer should, if necessary, be called in to fill the gap. Needless to say, it won't be in the least necessary. Joyce seemed to approve of my suggestion and it means, in effect, that Eric and Crispin will re-arrange things as we go along. That will suit Crispin and, with any luck, we shan't have any more truck from him.'

'So, despite all your good intentions, Myrtle's cause has now sunk like a stone and scarcely a ripple remains?'

'I'm afraid so. I feel bad about it because she was a game old thing and deserved better. It's bad enough having your career shot to pieces for all the usual reasons, but it must be worse still to feel that you have been brought down by supernatural forces.'

'So I had better tear this up,' Robin said, taking a white card from his pocket.

'Tear what up? What is it?'

'Something that arrived on my desk this morning, with a note from the President of the Alibi Club.'

'Heavens! Not another dinner?'

'Nothing so festive. Just an admission card for two. It should have been sent here really, but all my dealings with him have been through the office, so I suppose that's the only address he has.'

'Admission to what?'

'The Myrtle Sprygge Memorial Service.'

'Oh, dear! Where and when?'

'At the church of St John the Evangelist in Soho on the twenty-second of next month.

He explained that tickets are available on application, but that since you and I were present in a rather special capacity at her last public appearance and she had obviously enjoyed meeting us, it would be appreciated if we could be there. Very courteous.'

'Although I daresay you don't feel it puts you under any obligation to go?'

'No, I don't quite see myself skipping out on a working morning to spend a couple of hours in a Soho church. I suppose most of those who do will be writers, so it wouldn't matter to them. How about you?'

'I don't know. Perhaps I will go, just to make my apologies to the departed for ignoring her last request. Don't tear it up just yet, anyway.'

9

The letter, as dictated at second hand by Joyce, duly arrived and thereafter everything proceeded in accordance with the most optimistic predictions. Inevitably, there were occasional sparks and sulks from Crispin, but Eric handled him with admirable patience and tact and all of us who saw each day's rushes and then the rough cut at the end felt confident that, come the autumn, when it was scheduled for screening, his faith in the project would be amply justified. By 1 July I was out of work again.

This time, though, the situation was not so painful, as it might have been a gruelling three weeks enabling me for once to look forward with equanimity to a period of enforced rest.

Furthermore, my agent, as she did not neglect to remind me, had been busy on my behalf and there were signs that the pipelines were getting nicely clogged. So I decided to put my cares aside and spend a few days with my cousin Toby, relaxing in the undemanding hurly burly of life at Roakes Common.

It was at this point, I recall, that events began to depart from the path which had been mapped out for them and to stray off, literally as well as figuratively, into uncharted land. The first intimations came as I was taking the Oxford turn-off from the M4, on my way to Roakes, where I turned up about an hour later.

'You're late,' Toby said. 'Another ten minutes and we should have been in trouble with Mrs Parkes. As it is, you just have time for one very small drink before lunch.'

'What's the rush? Is she cooking something special?'

'No, it's gala night at the Bingo this evening and she has an appointment at two o'clock in Storhampton, to get her hair washed. Don't ask me why. It won't look any different when it's done and they have plenty of hot water in their flat, so it can't be that.'

Mrs Parkes is Toby's housekeeper and she and Mr Parkes, the gardener, live over the garage. During the dozen or more years of her iron rule, no one has ever seen her with a single misplaced hair in her puff of gold, except possibly Mr Parkes.

'Where have you been, anyway?' Toby asked. 'She insisted on telephoning your house just now and Mrs Cheeseman told her you'd left two hours ago.'

'Yes, I did, but I lost my way.'

'Oh yes, well, that's understandable, I suppose. It must be getting on for a month since you were last here and I daresay the landscape has changed quite a lot since then.'

'It may have, I didn't notice. The point is that I'd heard some shattering news on the car radio and my mind wandered. Before I knew it, I was stuck in the wilds of Maidenhead, which happens to be a very difficult place to get out of.'

'I believe you. Having tricked you into going there, they would naturally be reluctant to lose you again. What was the news? On second thoughts, you had better tell me over lunch. You may bring your drink with you, if it's not quite finished.'

'You shall have it in one sentence,' I told

him. 'Early this morning a woman was found dead from head injuries in the kitchen of her London home.'

'How very unpleasant! Anyone I know?'

'No, but you've heard of her often enough during the past few weeks. Her name was Gwen Montgomerie.'

'Are you sure? I find it hard to believe.'

'So did I and it's no wonder I lost all sense of direction. It was the wrong woman, you see. Now, if it had happened to Joyce, I should instantly have assumed that, egged on by me, she was beginning to make a nuisance of herself by throwing a spanner into Gwen's lovely plan for peddling other people's work. So, after thinking it over for a bit, Gwen decided to plunge her last penny on hiring some thugs to remove this fly from her ointment.'

'Perhaps that's more or less what did happen, only the thugs got the wrong woman?'

'I doubt it. She was killed in her own house, don't forget, and it's not very likely that Joyce would still be staying there. There would have been no need for it, once Eric had accepted the fact that Gwen would take no part in revising the script or sitting in at rehearsals. They'd need to have been very thick thugs indeed to have got it as wrong as all that.'

'Well, whatever the reason, perhaps it is all for the best. You might have felt responsible, if Joyce had been killed.'

'The trouble is, Toby, that I do feel responsible. You may call this silly and vain. . . .'

'Oh, may I?'

'But I can't help feeling that this might not have happened, if I hadn't stuck my oar in. I seem to have used it to stir up a hornets' nest and the really annoying part is that I haven't the faintest idea who the hornet is, or what kind of nest he is building.'

'No, I don't call that silly and vain.'

'What a relief!'

'Conceited and megalomanic are two of the words which would describe it better. What's it got to do with you that a woman you've scarcely met gets bashed over the head? And what possible connection could it have with your hinting to her husband's secretary that she should stop pirating other people's scripts?'

'Oh, I don't know, Toby. I just thought it was rather a heavy coincidence that it

135

should have happened at this particular time.'

'Well, I don't and neither would you, if you could stop seeing everything in terms of a three act drama, with you as the star. You can be quite sure that there was plenty going on in her life of which you were entirely ignorant and will never hear about. Did they give any details of this attack?'

'No, only the bare outline, but there'll be plenty more to come. I can't see the media failing to make capital out of the fact that her husband was a celebrated crime writer. We're sure to get the full story on the news tonight.'

'No, we shan't.'

'Why not? Have you carried out your lifelong threat to have the television removed?'

'We shall be dining out tonight.'

'Shall we really. Who with?'

'You remember those tiresome Grimbolds, who used to live at the house they re-named White Gables?'

'Yes, I do. Have they come back?'

'No, Portugal has swallowed them up, I am thankful to say, but White Gables has changed hands again.'

136

'Oh yes, you told me there was a new lot moving in, I remember now. Who are they?'

'A couple called Angostura, or some name like that. Mrs Parkes will know, if you're interested.'

'Why should I be interested?'

'Because it is they who have invited us for dinner.'

'And you accepted? Without even knowing their name? How very unlike you!'

'It was all a dreadful misunderstanding. They arrived, as you know, when I was staying with you and Robin in London. They had a little difficulty in finding out how to turn the water on at the main and finally appealed to Parkes, who just happened to be working in that corner of the garden which is but a shout away from theirs. He saw to the matter for them, whereupon Mrs Parkes, apparently considering that this gave her the entrée, seized the chance to hurry over with a pot of tea and a home-made cake. They were so grateful that they have been pestering me ever since to go and dine with them.'

'I should have thought it would be more appropriate to have invited the Parkes for dinner?'

'You would, wouldn't you? Unfortunately, opportunists are rarely awarded with the appreciation they deserve from other opportunists.'

'All the same, I still don't understand why you should have felt it necessary . . . Oh, hang on a minute, I see it now! Mrs Parkes is going to the Bingo gala and you would rather dine with people who bore you than put up with one of my omelettes?'

'That was a consideration, admittedly, but not the only one. I was thinking mainly of you.'

'A likely tale, but since you have got me into it, perhaps it would be as well to find out their name, after all. I can't address them as Mr and Mrs Angostura the whole evening.'

'You won't have to. On the numerous occasions when she has called here to beg for my presence at her table, I have learnt a good deal of their life history and I also know that they are called Ritchie and Helena. That is as much as you need. You have to be intimate friends with people of their sort for at least a decade before you find out their surnames.'

'Oh, really? Well, personally, I'm not too

keen on instant, oven-ready chumminess and I don't see that you were doing me a favour at all. I'd just as soon stay here and eat one of my own omelettes.'

'Oh, Tessa, how you do go on! I had a lovely surprise lined up for you, but all this argument about omelettes has trapped me into giving it away.'

'Giving what away? What surprise?'

'When I told you I had heard their life story it was no exaggeration, and my plan this evening was to walk in and say: 'Good evening, Helena. Allow me to introduce my cousin, Tessa, who was such a great friend and admirer of your Aunt Myrtle!'

10

'What does Ritchie do for a living?' I enquired, as we covered the hundred yards
which separated Toby's house from the front
door of White Gables.

'I have no idea, I have never spoken to
him. Something boring, I expect. Engineer,
or chartered accountant, probably.'

'Surely, Helena must have told you?'

'Yes, I'm sure she must, but I have a
discriminating memory and it is bound to
be something boring, otherwise I wouldn't
have forgotten.'

If he really pursued either of these occu-
pations, he was a master of disguise, for he
was an emaciated, scholarly looking man of
about forty, round shouldered and with a
few wisps of nondescript hair floating about
on his skull-like head. I could not tell
whether I would have allowed him to char-
ter an account for me, but I did know that I

should have strong reservations about walking over any bridge which he had constructed.

Helena, in contrast, was as flamboyant, in her different way, as her Aunt Myrtle. She had dark hair, straight and flowing, and was draped in a sage green velvet tea gown, with a chain round her neck supporting a heavy, square medallion of some modish ethnic origin.

The drawing room provided some surprises too. In Grimbold days it had epitomised the very essence of tasteless comfort, with two inch pile carpeting, cavernous chintzy armchairs and satin cushions, knick-knacks and occasional tables galore. All this had now been banished and high thinking and plain living had taken over. The curtains and upholstery were made of some material resembling dried porridge and the chairs were streamlined and angular. No longer were the walls adorned with ornately framed reproductions of Van Gogh and Renoir paintings, and in their place were floor to ceiling steel bookcases. A glowing fire, with quite a lot of dust on the brown and red logs, looked lost and forlorn in the inglenook fireplace and there was not even a vase of pampas grass on the grand piano, which occupied about a third of the floor space.

It struck me that the only possible explanation for this inappropriate decor was that they had bought the house during a fit of absent-mindedness, having confused Roakes Common with Hampstead Heath, and had thereafter compromised by creating a refuge in one corner of an Oxfordshire field, which would be forever London NW3.

This solution must have imprinted itself so firmly on my mind that during dinner, which was vegetarian and whose main course, by a startling coincidence, consisted of a somewhat leaden omelette wrapped around a stodge of pulses and root vegetables, I heard myself asking:

'I suppose you must have been living within a stone's throw of Myrtle before you moved down here? Did you see much of her?'

'Well, not all that close, actually,' Helena replied. 'Ritchie and I had a little house in Blackheath in those days. Do have some more wine, Toby. It is Ritchie's pride and joy.'

It was hard to see why because it was

served in a plain, bistro-type carafe, having first been decanted from a huge glass container, which had plainly started life in a chemist's shop, and Toby said he was rather off wine at present.

'Ah, yes, Blackheath,' I repeated, 'so not all that far away, either,' thinking that it would do just as well as Hampstead for the purposes of my theory.

'Although I can't say that we saw as much of her as I should have liked. In fact, I am afraid you have touched a rather sensitive nerve there, Tessa.'

'Oh, sorry! It was not intentional.'

'And in no way your fault. I blame myself entirely; but I regard remorse as such a self-indulgent, destructive emotion and I do rather despise myself for succumbing to it, where Myrtle was concerned.'

'You feel remorseful about her?'

'Not any more, I am happy to say. I can at least pride myself on having worked that ridiculous vanity out of my system, but I have to confess that I did go through that tiresome period of wishing I'd been able to do more for her, when I heard she'd died so suddenly, and all alone too, poor old dear. But there were problems, you know. She had no car, which made it difficult for her to get over to see us and I was always so selfishly engrossed in my work . . .'

'You mean you're a career woman?'

'Oh heavens, no, my dear. The nine to five routine is not my idea of the good life, but mine is a very absorbing occupation, for all that I do allow it to take over rather too much of my time and energy.'

'Helena is an artist,' Ritchie explained, 'and a very talented one, although she'll be furious with me for saying so.'

This was true, for she threw a lot of fury into scolding him for being so ridiculously biased.

'What kind of artist?' I enquired when she had calmed down.

'Collages, mainly,' Ritchie said, snatching the stick again in this relay race for two. 'However much she may protest, I shall insist on your both seeing some of her work after dinner, if you'd be interested.'

'Oh, most interested,' Toby declared. 'It must be ages since I saw a really decent collage.'

'She writes a bit too, as it happens. Working on a translation of Fernandez Villieros at present. You've heard of him, I expect?'

'I'm afraid not,' I admitted.

'Nothing to be ashamed of. Not an awful lot of people have in this country. He was a well-known Peruvian poet of the late nineteenth century, but his work has never so far been translated into English, curiously enough.'

'What a shame!' I said, hoping this would dispose of the subject, but Helena still had a few more shortcomings of her own to bring to our attention:

'Goodness knows when it will get finished. A labour of love, but uphill work, my Spanish being so rusty these days.'

'Yes, that must make it very hard for you,' Toby agreed solemnly, 'I marvel at your courage in attempting it at all.'

'I expect it was a challenge?' I suggested, before she could say so herself. 'And I daresay writing is in the blood, which must make all the difference.'

'In the blood?'

'Runs in the family. Myrtle, for example.'

'Oh yes, Myrtle, I'm with you now. Rather a different genre, of course, but it's true. She was very popular in her day.'

'And still is, I gather. Lots of paperbacks around.'

145

'Are there really? Well, that's nice to know, although I'm afraid the creative period, if one can use that term here, was over long ago. It must be years now since a new one came out. Poor Myrtle, one can understand how bitter she must have felt, after being a celebrity in her small way. I daresay it accounted for her general oddity in later life.'

'Quite a charming sort of oddity, though, wouldn't you agree?'

'My dear Tessa, you must be a good deal more tolerant than I am, or else you didn't know her very well, because I can't tell you the things she used to get up to. And living all alone in that dreadful cluttered basement, where everything looked as though it had been lumped together for an auction sale. I confess that was one reason why I . . . well, I won't say neglected her exactly, because I made a point of keeping in touch, but why I didn't do as much for her as I might have done. One felt it would be so tiring for her to come all the way out to Blackheath, just to have lunch with Ritchie and me. She'd probably have been bored to tears, but at the same time it would have been rather risky to invite other people to meet her. She was such a prickly person and she'd become a real eccentric in her old age, poor darling. Not that I have anything against eccentrics, per se,' she added, turning to Toby. 'In fact, Ritchie and I make a habit of collecting them.'

'Yes, I suppose their prickles do seem less offensive when one is not related to them,' he conceded.

'Including remarks of that sort,' Helena said, with coy reproach. 'How cruel of you to put me down like that! However, I shall forgive you and let you into a little secret. The reason for refusing to let you off coming to dinner with us had nothing to do with your being a famous playwright, believe it or not.'

'It never occurred to me that it had.'

'Well, thank you for that much, anyway. I should hate you to think of me as just another of those vulgar lion hunters, of which you must have more than your fill in a place like this. No, my real reason was that it had come to my ears that you were a bit of an eccentric yourself and that was quite irresistible. Is it true?'

'If it were, I suppose I should be the first to deny it.'

'The perfect answer! And I shall drink to it,' she said, raising her glass, 'and, hopefully, to the many future occasions when I shall have the pleasure of being put in my place by you!'

'And I suppose, even without being a lion hunter, you must have known your celebrated ex-uncle-in-law?' I asked, less to divert her attention from the fact that Toby's response to her toast had been confined to lifting his glass one inch from the table than to wrench the conversation back to Myrtle, despite all her attempts to slide away from it. Her description of her aunt had been so unlike the sharp-witted, humorous creature I had been lunching with a few days before her death that I was anxious to probe a little deeper into these recollections.

'William Montgomerie, you mean? Yes, indeed, but I was quite young at the time. That was in her heyday of course and she never had much success after they parted. The word went round in the family that her books were really written by him, but then we know what families are, don't we, Toby?'

'I think we are beginning to,' he admitted.

'All the same, you did know him,' I persisted, 'and perhaps also that poor Gwen who's now been murdered? I gather all three of them remained on good terms after he re-married.'

In introducing Gwen into the scenario, however, I had defeated my own purpose, for Helena seized on this item, clutching her head and exclaiming in horror and amazement:

'Murdered? Gwen murdered, did you say? But you can't be serious! Good God, what am I saying? As though you would joke about such a thing! But how did it happen? Who did it?'

'No one seems to know, or if they do they're not telling. We watched the six o'clock news this evening, but there wasn't much. Just that the house had been broken into by an unknown assailant and that she'd been killed by a single blow on the back of the head. Nothing about the weapon, only that the police were asking anyone who'd noticed anything out of the ordinary, like an unfamiliar car parked nearby, to be so good as to drop in and tell them about it. I am sorry to spring it on you, but I felt sure you'd have heard already.'

'We don't have a television set in the

house,' Helena said, this proud boast evidently doing much to restore her morale, 'and there was nothing about it in the morning paper. What a hideous shock, though! I hardly knew her, but she always seemed such a quiet inoffensive young woman. Curiously enough, the thing I remember best about her is that she always seemed to spend such hours in the hairdresser.'

'So I've heard. It's curious, in a way.'

'Oh, I don't know. She started out in the hairdressing business herself, I believe, so I daresay it was the only sort of ambience where she felt truly at ease. Oh dear, one really ought not to say such unkind things, now that she's dead. I really feel deeply distressed. She was the very last person one would associate with that kind of violence.'

'Although, to be fair, the violence was not on her side,' Toby reminded us. 'Hers was the passive role and I suppose we should take what comfort we can from that.'

Possibly Helena found this philosophical view to be somewhat too eccentric for even the most dedicated collector to take in her stride, for she responded by looking pensive and then, after a decent interval, suggesting to Ritchie that he should clear the plates and bring on the sweet.

I shall not attempt to describe what it consisted of, for I too have a discriminating memory, when it suits me, but I do recall that no further reference was made to Gwen, which effectively ruled out the chance of hearing more about Myrtle either.

I was later able to assure Toby, however, that his sacrifice had not been all in vain, for the evening had still to provide one more fascinating insight into the character of our hostess.

This came during a ten minute session with Ritchie in the attic, now converted into a studio, whose only light came from a north facing dormer window and a skylight which had been let into the ceiling. Toby had managed to extricate himself from this pilgrimage on the grounds that Dr Macintosh had told him that he would be ill advised to climb stairs after a heavy meal and Helena, aware no doubt that Ritchie's rapturous praise and enthusiasm for her ghastly collages would sound better in her absence, had elected to stay below and keep him company.

'She'd run a mile sooner than have it said in her hearing,' Ritchie said, 'but I think you'll agree that they do have rather a brilliant and original quality.'

Luckily, the daylight was now fading rapidly, so I was able to pour out the entire store of claptrap which I had memorised for ordeals of this sort, secure in the knowledge that it would not need to be stretched over more than five or six minutes.

'Oh, absolutely! Original is the very word I was looking for. And stark too, I think. There is a starkness about them, which I find curiously arresting. Does she ever show them in public?'

'Well, no, not often. That is always the great stumbling block with Helena. She simply cannot stand people gawping at her work. I did once manage to persuade her to mount a show in our local gallery at Blackheath, but she was a bundle of nerves for weeks before the vernissage and when the day came she'd absolutely made up her mind that she couldn't bear to part with a single one. She'd had red stickers put on the lot and so there wasn't much point in repeating the experiment. People naturally tend to feel cheated if everything has been sold before they get a sight of it.'

'What a shame! I suppose, if you're very

sensitive it must be awful to have people tramping round and passing judgement on works they have no understanding of, but perhaps they wouldn't all be raving philistines and I think you ought to try and persuade her to be a bit more thick skinned.'

'I've been trying for years,' Ritchie said, beginning, to my relief, to stack the pictures back against the walls, 'and I've got absolutely nowhere. The real trouble is that this diffidence, fastidiousness, call it what you like, is ingrained in her nature. It governs every aspect of her life and it's too late to try and eradicate it now.'

'I expect you'd know best about that,' I said, wondering for a terrible moment whether we had been talking about the same woman.

'You sound sceptical, but it's true, I assure you, and to prove it I'll give you an example. You remember that you and she were talking at dinner about her Aunt Myrtle, who died not long ago?'

'Yes, I do, although . . . .'

'You were going to say?'

'I'm probably wrong, but I had the impression that she found the subject boring, or distasteful in some way.'

'Which perfectly illustrates my point. I who know her so well can assure you that she was far from bored and that her distaste was due solely to the fact that she was afraid, above all, of sounding boastful, or of seeming to claim more credit than she deserved.'

'Was it really?'

'That must sound strange to you, but it is the truth. She told you, as I recall, that she felt ashamed to remember how little she had been able to do for her aunt during the last years?'

'Yes, she did.'

'Well, it was nonsense. Admittedly, Myrtle rarely came to see us in Blackheath. That was partly for the reasons Helena gave you, but largely, I suspect, because she didn't wish to inflict her ageing, cranky old relative on me. That doesn't mean, though, that Myrtle was in any sense neglected. On the contrary, my dear, unselfish wife was quite unstinting with her own time and concern. She used to go up to town at least once a month to spend the whole day with her aunt, and quite often she would stay the night as well, so that they could go to a play or concert together. There now, does that alter your view of her?'

'More than you'd ever guess,' I assured him, 'and I am so glad you told me.'

11

The media did their best, but the material was pitifully meagre. Heavy reference was made in the newspapers to the poignancy of a woman meeting her death in a manner so imitative of a scene in one of her husband's novels, and in the television news bulletin the same photograph of the exterior of the house in South Park Terrace was flashed on to the screen for about four times in as many hours. We were also treated to a number of blown up snapshots of Gwen at various stages of development, from the age of six months right through to her wedding, twelve years before her death.

One trouble was that, apart from this distinction, her life appeared to have been singularly uneventful. She seemed to have had few friends and no relatives at all, except for her elderly parents, who were seen squashed, somewhat unnaturally, side by side on a small couch in their terrace house in Stoke-on-Trent, in order to announce to the nation that they were very shocked by this terrible crime and appealed to whomever was responsible to give himself up.

Details of the murder itself, or such of them as the police chose to reveal, were equally thin on the ground. The house had been broken into, by way of a basement window, at some time between two and four a.m. and she had been killed by a single blow, struck from behind. No trace of the weapon had so far turned up, either in the house or garden, or in the gardens of neighbouring houses.

'Probably chucked it in the lake in Regent's Park,' I suggested.

'If so, it should narrow the field of suspects to manageable proportions,' Toby replied, 'for he must be the world champion caber tosser. The park gates are locked from dusk till dawn.'

'Yes, I suppose you're right. So presumably he took whatever it was away with him and dumped it somewhere else. It's odd, though, because one would have thought that even carrying a heavy object like that to the spot where he'd left his getaway car, if he had one, would have been risky. Not many people around at that hour, but all the more reason to be noticed and remembered by someone coming home late, or letting the cat out. However, that's for the police to busy themselves with and, personally, I'm more interested in what I'd call the domestic side. For instance, what was she doing in the kitchen at that hour of night?'

'I understand the theory is that she'd heard someone moving about and had come down to investigate.'

'And a right daft one too, in my opinion. She is reputed to have been such a timid, mouse-like creature. Everyone is agreed on that and I must say that the only time I ever saw her that's exactly how she struck me. So how do you reconcile that with hearing a noise in the middle of the night and prancing downstairs, unarmed, to find out what the intruder was up to? And anyway why the kitchen? What would he be doing in there?'

'Presumably, she thought that was where the noise was coming from.'

'Then it was a funny thought, is all I can say. Or, if true, he must have been a funny sort of burglar. What would he have expected to find in the kitchen that was worth stealing?'

'Who said anything about a burglar?'

'I don't know, Toby. I suppose I just took it for granted that was his game.'

'I can't imagine why. There's been no mention of stolen property, or the house being ransacked.'

'So you think more likely a rapist, or one of those?'

'Yes, naturally. And don't say "funny sort of rapist" because I don't know of any other sort. In fact, this one appears to have been cut strictly to pattern. Women who live alone are the natural targets and I can't remember hearing of one who didn't use a basement window as the means of entry.'

'Then all the more strange of Gwen to have gone dashing downstairs to meet him half way. Wouldn't you have expected her to jump out of bed, lock the door and then dial 999? Or, failing that, to stick her head under the bedclothes and pray he would go away?'

'Yes, in some circumstances, but there could be others to account for her not doing so.'

'Name a few!'

'All right, if I must. Let us say she is woken by a noise, breaking glass, perhaps, which she vaguely associates with something or someone outside in the street, such as a milk bottle being kicked over. However, there is no further sound, the intruder by this time being inside the house and padding around to get his bearings. Unfortunately, though, she is one of those people who, woken after a few hours sleep, are doomed to spend the next two or three hours wide awake. So what more natural than to go down to the kitchen to make herself a hot drink?'

'Yes, I see what you mean. In fact, I can't find any flaw at all in that argument.'

'Good! So that disposes of that.'

'No, it doesn't. On the contrary, Toby, we are only just beginning. If your reconstruction is correct, why did he kill her?'

'Oh well, because she resisted his advances, I suppose, or began to scream and he went berserk.'

I shook my head: 'No, that won't do. There's been no mention of a struggle and, anyway, she was struck from behind. You can't put up a very stiff resistance against someone when you've got your back to him.'

'Then we must change the script and make him not a common-or-garden rapist, but a homicidal maniac, a sort of Regent's Park Jack-the-Ripper, whose mission in life is to exterminate solitary women on the grounds that they're more likely than not to be prostitutes. However, I gather from your mulish expression that you don't like that theory any better?'

'You're dead right, I don't. From what I know about such people, which I'm happy to say is very little, one thing is clear. They don't go about the extermination business in that way at all. Strangling and mutilation and unmentionable things of that kind are what they get their kicks from. A nice clean swipe from behind would be as dull as a wet Sunday afternoon. There wouldn't even be the fun of seeing the agonised expression on the victim's face.'

'Well, if you are determined to adopt this negative attitude, I regret that I can be of no further use to you. Perhaps Robin will be able to provide you with something more to your liking. Failing that, it looks as though you will have to contain your curiosity until such time as the police manage to track this man down and tell you all about it.'

'I doubt if they will manage to. I suspect they'll be looking in all the wrong places for all the wrong reasons. Besides, curiosity doesn't come into it. I have a strong feeling that there must be some connection between this murder and what has gone before.'

'Somehow I thought you would.'

'Well, tell me honestly, Toby, don't you find it an extraordinary coincidence that all three of the people nearest the heart of matters should have dropped off, one by one, during the past six months?'

'Not in the least. Two were elderly, of whom one suffered from a chronic heart condition. The other died, I understand, from that very complaint that Dr Macintosh has been warning me about for years and which people who drink and smoke and otherwise enjoy themselves in ways in which I feel certain Willie Montgomerie did, are specially prone to. I grant you that the circumstances of this third death are a little unusual, but by no means unheard of.'

'All right, so it's my turn now and I shall tell you why I find all your rational arguments so unconvincing. You say that Willie's death followed naturally from the life he led, but we should not forget either that it came at a very convenient time for Gwen, nor that he was taken ill at home and remained there until he was past help and about to die.'

'It is no good saying I shouldn't forget these things. I have never heard them mentioned before. In what way did it come at a convenient time for Gwen?'

'The financial one, mainly. He was tending more and more to neglect his novels, which is what his income had always come from, in favour of films and television, where he was comparatively unknown. There was also the fact that the lease on the house was running out and it must have seemed to her to be a particularly unfortunate time to throw away security and take off into such a chancy world.'

'No reason why he wouldn't have made a success of it. Judging by most of what one has to sit through, it doesn't require any special talent.'

'Ah, but that raises another question. Supposing he had brought it off, how much of his success, do you imagine, would have rubbed off on Gwen? It was one thing when he was working flat out at home all day and quite content, at the end of it, to sit down to the cosy little dinner she had prepared for him and hear all the latest gossip at the hairdresser's. But, if you ask me, his venture into show biz had gone to his head. It had opened up a new and exciting world for him, in which Gwen had no part at all. I spent a good deal of time with him, one way and another, during the production, sometimes with other people and sometimes on our own and he never once mentioned Gwen or behaved as though he had a home of his own to go back to. I didn't even realise he was married until I read the obituary and I can't see that Gwen had much to look forward to. She could well have begun to see that he had reached the dangerous age and the only safe place for him was in his coffin.'

'It's a biggish step from that to coming up with a plan to put him there.'

'Quite so, but it is one which has sometimes been taken and, like so many mild little females, Gwen was very money conscious and also very ruthless. We can tell that from the way she lost no time in pinching Myrtle's script and putting her own name on it. And, talking of Myrtle, there's another funny thing.'

'I hope it is funnier than the last one, which has slightly depressed me.'

'It has nothing to do with Gwen, if that's your worry. Nor Willie either, as far as I can see, although I am sure there must be a connection, if only I can find it. It emanates from your new friends and neighbours.'

'Oh God, not the Angosturas? They depress me even more. Do you suppose I'll have to ask them back?'

'Oh, certainly. You had better make it next Saturday, when Robin has promised to try and get down.'

'I can't see him having very much in common with them. I very much doubt if Ritchie can tell a golf club from a flat iron and Robin probably thinks a collage is something you wear round your neck.'

'Don't underestimate him. And anyway, it's not artistic appreciation I'm after. He is used to dealing with psychopaths and liars and people pretending to be what they're not and I want him to tell me which category Helena belongs in.'

'I didn't see her pictures, of course, but were they really as bad as that?'

'Oh, absolutely! No one with a balanced mind could possibly have executed them.

Although I am not actually accusing her of madness. Or, if so, it's probably the kind with method in it. I am specially interested to know why she told us such a string of lies about her Aunt Myrtle.'

'Yes, I noticed that her description did not quite tally with the one you and Robin had given me of that forceful old party twirling around in crimson caftan.'

'It was outrageous. Myrtle was no more a doddering old crank than you are. Rather less so, in fact. Anyone would conclude that Helena hadn't set eyes on her for the last twenty-five years.'

'Which must be the answer. She most likely hadn't troubled to set eyes on her for the last twenty-five years, but the need to preserve her own image, as what she would no doubt describe as a warm and caring person, prevented her admitting it. Taking a chance on the fact that Myrtle's age, combined with her chronic heart condition and inability to write novels any more would add up to advanced senility, she announced it to be so. It was a natural mistake.'

'Just what I thought and should have gone on thinking, if Ritchie hadn't been so eager to impress on me that he was married to the doyenne of all the martyred saints. It just goes to show what harm people can do to each other with good intentions. He insisted that Helena used to visit her aunt regularly in London. At least once a month, he said, and quite often she stayed the night, only she refused to talk about it, preferring her good deeds to be done by stealth and out of the vulgar public gaze. Can you believe it?'

'It certainly does seem to be carrying modesty to an excessive degree.'

'And I'm sure he believed what he was saying too, and yet Myrtle never breathed a word about this devoted, attentive niece. I know that doesn't prove anything, but, one way and another, she talked a hell of a lot about her life and times and she gave the impression that, towards the end, Gwen was the one who stood by and rallied in an emergency.'

'All the same, she did omit to tell you that she had formerly been married to Gwen's husband.'

'Yes, you're right, Toby, I have to admit it. On the other hand, she may have assumed that I knew already. People who are celebrities in their own small world don't always realise how small it is.'

'Well, it's a teaser about Helena, I agree, although I can't see how knowing the answer would help you in finding out who killed Gwen.'

'Just the same, it might be worth pursuing, if the chance arises. And another thing I must find out is how Mrs Parkes stands in the matter of vegetarian cooking.'

'Oh, you don't need to bother about that. We have faced this situation before and she has it all at her finger tips. There will be extra Yorkshire pudding for those who don't want beef and she makes the best avocado soup you've ever tasted. No one would ever guess that it was not based on the finest chicken stock.'

12

Not a single Harman in the directory had the right prefix and those with a plain J. in front of them lived at such improbable sounding addresses that I rejected them all and, on impulse, telephoned the house in South Park Terrace. It was one worth obeying because on the tenth ring, when I had all but replaced the receiver, I heard the faint cackle of her voice:

'Oh, Miss Harman!' I said, clamping it to my ear again. 'Is that you, Joyce?'

'Oh . . . er . . . yes. I was just leaving. How did you know I was here?'

'Took a chance. Have the police gone now?'

'Well, more or less. They've finished whatever they were doing, but they warned me they might be back.'

'Are you staying at the house?'

'Oh no, I don't think that I could bear to

do that. In fact, I've cleared everything out of my room here. But I come in every day. There's such a lot to see to and tidy up and there doesn't seem to be anyone else . . . .'

'How horrid for you!'

'Well, yes, it's not very pleasant, but the daily woman refuses to set foot in the place and I can't very well just walk out and shut the door on all this muddle.'

'But there's no hurry, is there? Can't you get the solicitors to lay on someone to come in next week and clear it up?'

'Well, yes, I suppose I could do that, although they don't seem keen to make any move at all. They keep saying that sort of thing must wait until the criminal side has been sorted out.'

'And can't it?'

'Oh well, you know how it is. At least, I hope you don't, but the fact is that it may take weeks and in the meantime . . . . Oh, I expect it sounds silly, but it's what people mean when they say that in the midst of life we're in death. Or do I mean the other way round? I'm so bad at expressing myself, that's my trouble. What I was trying to say was that, even when something tragic and horrifying on a grand scale like this has happened, you can't just close your eyes and ignore all the day-to-day business. You still have to deal with it, just as though everything was normal.'

'You mean like stopping the milk and newspapers? That kind of thing?'

'Well, yes, there's all those niggling little chores too, of course, but it's worse than that. I mean, I don't want to bore you with a lot of trivial details, but they sort of weigh on me. For instance, I found the laundry basket absolutely brimming over with dirty linen and clothes. There was even the pink dress she was wearing the last time I saw her. She always did the washing every Monday, come rain or shine, you see, so of course there was quite a pile and I can't just leave it there, can I?'

'Can't you?'

'I suppose, if I had any sense, I could, but it seems so unkind, so sort of unfeeling, in a way. Gwen would have hated anyone to see it like that and I feel I can't just walk out and leave it to some stranger to dispose of all her personal things. I'll have to take them home to wash and then pack them up for Oxfam, or something. And then there's the refrigerator.'

'What's the matter with the refrigerator?'

'Nothing, only I've been told to disconnect all the electric fittings when I leave, because of the fire risk, and it's absolutely chock full. Enough to last for a week and a lot more in the freezer section too. It seems such a crime to let it all go bad, but what can I do? I don't know what to do really. I can't just leave it there to rot, can I?'

'Why not take it home with you? Or don't you fancy that idea?'

'Well, no, not much. I don't mean I'm squeamish exactly, I suppose it would be silly to get sentimental over food, but I haven't got a big appetite and I can't see how I'd ever get through it. And anyway, there's far too much for my refrigerator to hold. There were six bottles of milk there, for a start. I did take two of those and the remains of a joint she'd had hot on Sunday. I don't know why she always bought so much, when the shops were only just round the corner and there was only herself and sometimes me left to cater for. Half the time she didn't even remember what she'd got in that old deep freeze she was so proud of.'

'How about the neighbours? Couldn't some of them give you a hand?'

'I don't think I'd dare ask them. They're probably furious about what's happened, anyway. You know, all the publicity and police cars and cameras blocking the whole street. Besides, Gwen was never on friendly terms with them. I doubt if she knew their names, even. You know how it is in cities?'

'No, I don't, as it happens. We're very chummy with most of ours, always telephoning each other to borrow parking space and send out warnings when we're going to have a party and so on.'

'Oh well, Gwen was very shy and reserved, you know. Not a bit like you . . . you're so very . . . Which reminds me, I've been talking all this time about my own troubles and I never asked you why you'd rung. I'm afraid there's nothing I can tell you about Gwen's . . . death . . . if that's what you . . . I mean your husband would probably know more about it than I do.'

'No, it had nothing to do with that and you're quite safe. I wouldn't dream of trying to pump you. I just wondered whether you intended to go to Myrtle Sprygge's Memorial Service?'

'Oh, I don't know . . . I haven't really

thought about it . . . Nigel did send me a card, but I don't suppose he cares whether I go or not, and anyway, that was before all this . . . I don't even remember the date.'

'Next Thursday. Today week, in fact.'

'Oh, I see. Will you and your husband be going?'

'Not Robin. He has to work and that's the snag. I'd like to go, but I shan't know a soul there, except Mr Banks, and I was thinking perhaps you and I might go together?'

She responded to this with the longest pause so far, and I hoped she was not going to point out that an intimate acquaintance with the rest of the congregation is not generally considered to be a prerequisite for these occasions. At last she said:

'I don't suppose I shall, either, but of course if you really think I'd be any help . . . I mean, I'm very flattered . . . It was kind of you to suggest it, but . . . .'

'Good! It starts at eleven, so I'll pick you up on my way, shall I?' I asked, hoping to scoop her up into my bulldozer before she could dodge out of the way. 'Just let me write down your address.'

It was somewhere just north of Holland Park, which, if not exactly on my way, was scarcely four miles out of it, and as soon as I had scribbled it down I rang off without giving her time to point this out.

'Or rather,' as I admitted a few minutes later to Toby, 'without giving her time to put a sentence to that effect together. She has a curious trick of starting by using words to convey the opposite of what she means, so it sometimes pays to attend to the words and ignore the meaning.'

'Not unlike Mrs Angostura in that respect?' he suggested.

'Yes, you're right in a way, only the motive is different. I think Joyce's equivocation comes from a compulsion to speak the truth, combined with a natural dislike of hurting people's feelings. I am sure Helena was never inspired by anything so good-natured. I only wish I did know what lay behind all her lies and pretences and now it doesn't look as though I'll get any help from Robin, after all. I forgot to tell you this, but there's something on and he doesn't see much hope of getting here until quite late on Saturday. Not in time for dinner, anyway.'

'Does Mrs Parkes know this?'

'Naturally. I wouldn't have forgotten to tell her.'

'Then perhaps it is just as well. The Angosturas are bringing an extra guest.'

'No! Who?'

'His name is Jim and he is an old friend of Ritchie's. They were at university together. That's about all I can tell you. It appears that Ritchie, who seems to be uncommonly vague for an engineer, had forgotten he'd been invited, but luckily Helena remembered just in time and during one of your interminable telephone calls she sailed over to ask if it would be all right to bring him to dinner.'

'I expect she only got the idea of inviting him when she knew there was a free dinner going and she forgot to tell Ritchie what she'd done. You had to say yes, of course?'

'I tried my best not to. I assured her that we shouldn't be in the least offended if she preferred to put us off until next weekend, or, better still, the one after, but she would have none of it. She would rather die than upset our arrangements, especially when Mrs Parkes had gone to all that trouble.'

'All what trouble?'

'You may well ask. Helena could hardly imagine that she would make the avocado soup forty-eight hours in advance. She simply says whatever comes into her head to get her own way, tiresome woman!'

'The timing was really rather shrewd, though. Just a little late to drop out altogether, but plenty of time to make sure there would be enough for Jim. Did she tell you what his other name was, by any chance?'

'She may have, but I wasn't listening. As we shall be required to address him as Jim the minute he enters the house, it hardly seemed worth bothering about.'

'And besides, it wouldn't really help to know it.'

'Haven't I just said so?'

'You have, but I was thinking of something else. I have an idea that Myrtle once mentioned someone called Jim. At any rate, I associate the name with her, but as I don't know what that one's surname was either, there'd be no way of telling whether they're the same man.'

'Well, you could ask him I suppose, and that would give Helena the chance to leap in and reproach herself all over again for having neglected her poor, feeble-minded old auntie.'

'Yes,' I agreed, 'that is more or less what I had in mind to do.'

13

By half past ten the dinner party had broken up, which is to say that three of its members still remained round the dining room table, while Helena and I had been banished to the drawing room. This arrangement was in accordance with Toby's advance instructions and had been carried out much against my will. I did not think Helena would take kindly to being deprived of three quarters of her audience at one sweep, and nor did she. In fact, having studiously ignored all my nods and becks and wreathed smiles, in the end her departure had only been effected by a ruse.

'Oh, Tessa, are you on the move?' Toby enquired seeing what I was up against and standing up himself. Whereupon Helena also stood up and followed me to the door. I had ushered her out of the room before she realised that he had sat down again.

'Dear me, what a quaint, old fashioned eccentric your cousin turns out to be,' she remarked sourly, as I handed her some coffee. 'I had a vague impression that you were trying to catch my eye, as people used to say in Edwardian novels, but I must confess that the significance escaped me. I had simply no idea that anyone still kept up these antiquated, chauvinist customs of segregating the sexes in what is supposed to be a civilised gathering. Don't you find it quite extraordinary?'

I regard myself as one of the most ardent feminists in existence, but for some reason whenever I am in the presence of an active crusader in the field my enthusiasm is apt to wane and I said:

'Cheer up, I don't suppose they'll be very long, and in the meantime it gives us a chance to talk on our own, and I'm dying to ask you about your friend Jim. I couldn't get a word out of him. I was finally reduced to asking him whether he knew this part of the country well and he said he didn't. Is he always so dour and silent?'

'Not that I know of. He's really more Ritchie's friend than mine, but I've never had much difficulty in finding things to say to him when we do meet.'

This I could believe, but it did not quite answer the question and I tried again:

'Well, I expect I'm not quite up to his intellectual standard. What does he do for a living?'

'A variety of things. He is a man of many parts. But I don't think that knowledge would have helped you very much. For instance, he used to be a successful Harley Street doctor.'

'Oh, really? A specialist?'

'No, physician. I believe he originally intended to specialise in heart disease, but other things cropped up. What a magnificent show those sweet peas make! From the garden, I suppose? I wish we had something like that in ours, but it has been so dreadfully neglected and there is far too much for Ritchie to cope with on his own.'

'What a shame! And to tell you the truth, I doubt if I could have managed to be very scintillating on medical subjects, either. Unlike actors, in my experience doctors and lawyers become uneasy when they are questioned about their work. They seem to take the attitude that they are being conned into giving away free professional advice, which is rather inhibiting.'

'Bitter experience, I daresay, although you'd have been less likely to run into that problem with Jim. He has virtually given up his practice now.'

'Yes, so you hinted. Rather young to re-tire, wasn't he? White hair can be deceptive in lots of ways, but even so, I'd have put him in his early fifties.'

'Quite near the mark. He and Ritchie are almost the same age.

'Is Ritchie a doctor too?'

'Oh, heavens no. He works with the ORRP, which stands for the Overseas Refugee and Rehabilitation Project, in case you didn't know. They do a lot of field work, but their headquarters happen to be in London. Didn't Toby tell you?'

'Oh yes, I believe he did, now you men-tion it. So I suppose he started by being a sociologist?'

'Well done, my dear!' Helena said, not bothering to conceal her amazement at this brilliant display of acumen, 'although he read archaeology when he first went up. He switched over in his second year.'

'Oh well, I suppose the two sub-jects do have something in common.

How about Jim?'

'Jim? Good heavens, just look at the time! Do you suppose Toby means to keep the men out there for the rest of the evening?'

Since the truthful answer to this was in the affirmative, I decided to ignore it and plod on:

'Did Jim intend to become an archaeologist too, before he got sidetracked?'

'I am not sure that is quite the word to use in Ritchie's case, but I take your meaning, of course. No, so far as I remember, Jim was interested in the subject purely as an amateur, although he is remarkably well informed, I am told. As I said, he is a man of many parts.'

'Yes, you did, although you didn't say what the other parts were.'

'Well, he is a writer, among other things. He doesn't publish under his own name, of course.'

'Is he really? That's interesting. What kind of thing does he write? Beer swilling medical students, or struggling young GP's fighting the corrupt councillors in regional slums?'

'No, neither of those. His are science fiction, which is also very popular with the libraries, I understand.'

'And why doesn't he publish them under his own name?'

'My goodness, what a lot of questions! Do you make a habit of it?'

'Yes, I'm afraid I do, but you don't have to answer them, if you'd rather not. We could talk of something else.'

'Oh, I haven't the slightest objection, if it amuses you. We may just as well pass the time that way as any other. And I apologise if I sound ungracious. It's not that I don't enjoy the company of women. I assure you that in normal circumstances I find it immensely rewarding, but that is not quite the same, in my humble opinion, as the two of us being thrust out here to make the best we can of each other. Quite honestly, I find it all rather strange and archaic. However . . . What was it you asked me?'

'Why doesn't Jim publish under his own name?'

'Oh, I see! Well, the answer is quite simple. He took up writing when he was still in full time practice, so naturally he was compelled to use a pseudonym. You may not know this, but the BMA, the British Medical Association, that is, lays down very strict rules about that kind of thing.'

'So what name does he use?'

'Ormsby. It was his mother's name. I don't suppose you've even heard of him?'

'Yes, I think I have, although I'm sure I haven't read any of his books. Still, if he's well known, it must be a name one often sees in bookshops, so I suppose that would account for it.'

'Do I hear sounds of movement?' Helena asked sitting up straight and putting on an alert expression.

'Yes, but I'm afraid they're coming from the wrong direction. That's just Mrs Parkes, making the rounds before she goes home. Incidentally, I must warn her not to bolt the front door, in case Robin arrives after we've gone to bed. She'll have left the garden door unlocked for you, but he may not realise that.'

'Robin?'

'My husband. He's working late tonight, which is something which nearly always seems to happen at weekends. I hope you won't mind if I leave you for a minute and go and deal with it?'

'Is he in a show?'

I was on my feet by this time, but, bewildered by the question, stopped short and stared back at her:

'In a show? Well, no, obviously there's some fracas going on, but I don't think he would describe it as a show exactly. Rather more undercover than that.'

'Oh, excuse my ignorance, my dear. I seem to have jumped to the wrong conclusion. Naturally, I assumed that being your husband he would be on the stage too.'

Unable to see what was natural about it, I replied a trifle tartly, 'Oh dear me, no. Nothing could be wider of the mark. He is a detective inspector at Scotland Yard and the nearest he's ever been to a stage is the third row of the stalls. I'll be back in a moment.'

Evidently, however, even an audience of one was preferable to none at all, for she jumped up in great haste, saying:

'No, no, do let me go. There is something I particularly want to ask Mrs Parkes, while I have the chance. I'll put in a word about the front door, so not to worry.'

She darted from the room and remained outside until nearly ten minutes later, when, alerted no doubt by the male voice choir from the drawing room, she came speeding back, all smiles again, to tell us, what a gem Mrs Parkes was and how she would trade her soul to have someone like that, even for a few hours a week.

It availed her nothing, though, because Toby, having no designs on her soul, ignored the hint and a few minutes later, when she was barely launched on her next monologue, Jim made one of his rare entries into the conversation by remarking that it had been a long day and that he was an early riser.

'Oh, me too,' Toby agreed, which was a black lie, 'early to bed has always been the way of life here,' thereby twitching the rug from under Helena's feet and practically forcing her to drag herself and her party away.

My single regret about this abrupt departure was that it had deprived Ritchie of the chance to explain to me that Helena's reticence on the subject of the lugubrious Jim came from her terror of being praised for all the kindness she had heaped on him over the years.

14

'Mr and Mrs Anstruther are having a bit of an upper and downer this morning. Late nights don't suit them, I daresay,' Mrs Parkes announced when I sauntered downstairs in search of coffee soon after ten on Sunday morning.

Robin was still asleep, having collapsed into bed in the small hours and Toby had not yet put in an appearance either. In theory, the early mornings, Christmas Day included, are sacred to his work, although it had not escaped me that the Sunday papers were not on view either. Starved of news of the outside world, I made do with what was available.

'Who are Mr and Mrs Anstruther?' I asked, seating myself at the kitchen table.

'Well, you ought to know, seeing they were having dinner here only last night.'

'Oh, those people! Well, go on! How do

you know they're having an upper and downer this morning?'

'Heard them at it, didn't I? Not intentional, mind.'

'No, I'm sure. Were they having it in the garden?'

'No, in what they call their living room. I just dropped over, you see, to give her that recipe she'd asked for.'

'What recipe?'

'For the avocado soup. Didn't she tell you? She came flying out last night, when I was seeing to the windows and that, and started going on about what a real gourmet dish it was and how she wished she could make something as good as that. I was in a bit of a hurry to get home by then, what with Mr Crichton spinning it out like that in the dining room, and as it was I had to leave the port glasses till the morning. So anyway I said I'd write out the recipe for her and bring it over some time. Mind you, she's not much of a cook, by all accounts, so I daresay it won't turn out quite the same as mine.'

'No, I can see that it might lack a certain something. Did they start upping and downing after you'd given it to her?'

'Oh no, that came before and I wasn't intended to hear. It was just accidental, really, but I went through the garden, like I always do, that being the quickest, and I saw the glass door of the living room was open, so I guessed that was where I'd find her.'

'Oh, I get it! They were both in there and going at it full blast. Never mind, these things will occur when people are careless enough to leave doors open while they're having a row. I expect it was different in Blackheath.'

'It wasn't what you'd call a row exactly. He's such a quiet sort of chap, gives in to her left, right and centre as a rule, only this time he must have been digging his heels in a bit, but she was the one who was making all the noise.'

'What was it about?'

'Far as I could tell, it was some arrangement they'd made, which he'd gone and forgotten. That wouldn't surprise me. He's a very vague sort of man, you know. Always forgetting everything and then she has to remind him. Got his mind on higher things, I daresay, only this time, as I told you, he seemed to be standing up for himself. From the way she was going on about how she'd told him half a dozen times to write it down and how could he ever think she'd make a mistake like that, you could tell that's exactly what he did think.'

'What arrangement was it? Did you get that bit too?'

'Couldn't help it. You can't very well barge in on people when they're in that state and I've got enough to do, without running back and forth with recipes all day. It was something about how they'd made a plan to go and have lunch with these friends of theirs in Blackheath, to collect some stuff they'd left behind when they moved, and how they couldn't let them down at the last minute. It's a pity they ever did move, if you ask me. They don't fit in here and they don't seem to want to, either. I hear they turn up their noses at everyone, unless they have a title, or happen to be famous, like Mr Crichton. Oh, and another thing was that she said she knew she couldn't have mistaken the day because the idea was that they were going to take Jim to lunch there as well and then drop him off in Harley Street on their way home, to save him having to get a train back this evening.

And, if he didn't believe her, he could ring the people up himself and ask them. Very sharp, she was. Not a bit the way she'd talk to him in public.'

'And with some excuse, you have to admit. He must have been the one to get it wrong, particularly since he's known to be so absent-minded. The only puzzle is why he should have thought it worth arguing about.'

'Ah well!' Mrs Parkes said, looking mysterious and arch about it, 'The fact is, I think you may have something to answer for there.'

'Whatever can you mean? How could it possibly concern me?'

'Well, not you personally, perhaps, unless he's taken a fancy to you.'

'As well he might, considering the effort I put into raving about his wife's pictures, but I shan't let it give me ideas. I'm afraid his heart belongs to Helena.'

'Oh, you've seen those, have you? Dreadful, ugly things, aren't they? You'd think someone with all her advantages would find a better way to use her time.'

'Perhaps she would, if she didn't have so many advantages, but we're getting off the point. What made you say it was my fault that he was being so obstinate about this jaunt to Blackheath?'

'Well, it was difficult to make out, not being able to hear more than a quarter of what he said, but it sounded as though he'd made some arrangement for all of you to go over there and have a drink with them before lunch this morning.'

'Really? I hadn't heard anything about it.'

'Well, you wouldn't, would you? I expect it was something they cooked up while they were drinking their port and you know as well as I do that wild horses wouldn't drag Mr Crichton there when it came to the point, so he wouldn't have thought it worth mentioning to you. Anyway, when she heard that, she turned very scathing. Said it was something you could do any day of the week and it didn't have to be the one time when they'd promised to go and see some of their real friends. Then I think he must have said something about the Inspector and that really set her off.'

I considered it unlikely that Ritchie would have referred to Robin in this way, but, in her different fashion, Mrs Parkes picks her way over just as many eggshells as Toby, when it comes to names. In general, she does not approve of first names being bandied about between people in different walks of life, but on the other hand she prides herself on being up to date and realises that nowadays she might be ridiculed for sticking to the formalities, particularly with people she has known for years and who are younger than herself. She compromises by calling Robin the Inspector, which is descriptive, rather than subservient, and by calling me Tessa behind my back and You to my face. If we both survive to see the day, the problem will finally be resolved for her when I am made a dame.

'How did that set her off?' I enquired.

'She let out one of her squawky laughs, you know how she does, and she says: 'I suppose you know, my dear Ritchie, that he's a policeman? I never thought we'd be entertaining one of those in our home, but you please yourself. If that's becoming your idea of congenial company, you had better stay behind and enjoy it on your own." Those were her exact words, but you mustn't take offence, you know. She's very down on the police, but it's only because of that newspaper she reads,' Mrs Parkes explained, advancing an interesting theory as to how the opinions of the intelligentsia were formed.

'It doesn't bother me. How did Ritchie take it?'

'He didn't have time to take it, or not take it. The doctor must have come into the room while she was speaking. Dr Temple, that is, not our Dr Macintosh, and she changed her voice back to the ordinary and said: "Oh, Jim, we were just trying to decide what time we ought to leave for Blackheath." So I knew that was the end of it and I went in and gave her the recipe. What's the matter with you, then? Seen Hamlet's ghost again?'

'What did you say his name was?'

'Who's name?'

'Jim's.'

'Dr Temple. What's so peculiar about that?'

'I'll tell you one day, but how did you find out?'

'Told me herself, didn't she? Three or four days ago, when she came over to ask if it would be all right to pick one or two of the roses for her dining room table. "We've got an old friend, a Dr Temple, coming for the weekend, you see," she said. She doesn't use these familiarities with everyone, you know. Quite snobby underneath it all and it's "Mr Crichton" and "Mr Anstruther" when she's talking to me. Want some more coffee?'

What I most needed were a few wet towels round my head, to clear the brain, but I told her that coffee would do, to be going on with.

'I am sorry I missed the dinner party,' Robin said.

'You were lucky. It was tedious beyond belief. Helena spent the evening praising herself with faint damns, Ritchie filled in with the accompaniment and their guest behaved as though his appeal for a stay of execution had just been turned down.'

'I bet the roast beef was good, though?'

'There wasn't any beef. Mrs Parkes put her foot down over that.'

'Good for her! It's nice to know there's someone in this household who cares about the susceptibilities of vegetarians.'

'No, there isn't. She has a theory that roast beef is a winter dish and quite inappropriate for this time of year. It had to be

195

Welsh lamb. The poor Angosturas more or less had to make do with new potatoes and mint sauce.'

'How about dismal Jimmie? Was he a vegetarian too?'

'Half and half.'

'Oh well, that's a new twist, I suppose. How does it work in practice?'

'It was most mysterious. He seemed to be in a kind of daze most of the time. He almost shuddered when Toby offered him a cut off the joint, which was quite a reasonable reaction, except that later on he went and poured about half a pint of rich Parkes gravy all over his vegetables. I couldn't make it out.'

'I expect he is a poor simple bachelor, who didn't realise what had gone into the making of it.'

'Although, bachelor or not, he is reputed to be a successful doctor, so you wouldn't expect him to be as simple as all that. Unless, of course, Helena made it up, which would be quite in character, if she thought it would enhance her own prestige. Any news from the big city?'

'Oh yes, glad you reminded me. There was a message for you. The telephone started to ring just as I was locking myself out of the house last night and I had to go in again to answer it, in case it was your agent. She is one of the few people I know who wouldn't hesitate to ring you up at half past eleven at night.'

'Although there are others, apparently. Which one was it?'

'Eric.'

'Oh, really? Happy or unhappy?'

'Un. He wanted me to tell you that there's been a hitch. The screening has been postponed indefinitely.'

'Oh, hell! Why's that?'

'He has no idea. The directive came from above and he was given no details, except that it had something to do with probate and settling Gwen's estate. He wants you to telephone him when you get home and fix a date for lunch, so that you can both have a good cry about it. Or perhaps, if I'm interpreting correctly, because he has a shrewd idea that you might have more information on the subject than he has.'

'And I have a feeling he's right, although it wouldn't do to say so. Still, I don't mind having lunch with him and doing my bit of crying. It's always heartbreaking and frustrating when productions get shelved, for whatever reason, and you can't be sure whether after all the triumphs and disasters and hard slog they'll ever see the light of day. In the meantime, though, any developments on Gwen's murder?'

'Nothing much. Neither the weapon, nor anything resembling it, has so far come to light on the premises, or anywhere else, which is also fairly heartbreaking and frustrating, in its way.'

'When you say resembling, does that mean they have a fair idea of what they're looking for?'

'Nothing so positive, unfortunately. According to the medical evidence, the picture turns out to be something in the nature of a sledgehammer. Hardly the kind of implement you would expect to find in the average London kitchen.'

'And not the kind of thing, either, that one would expect to see someone lugging around in a well-heeled residential area at dead of night.'

'Not unless he had brought it with him and taken it away again in the same suitcase. But that would indicate that he had gone there with intent to commit murder, which effectively rules out all the more likely potential suspects. And in any case, why lumber himself with such a cumbersome weapon, when something just as effective could have been tucked into his coat pocket?'

'And anyway, they don't believe that it was premeditated?'

'Well, let's say there's no evidence to support that assumption. She was an unusually negative and reserved sort of woman, as you know, entirely wrapped up in her husband while he was alive, and people who don't inspire strong feelings are unlikely to acquire dangerous enemies. At any rate, if she did have one, he has managed to keep well hidden.'

'I know it's often been said that she had practically no friends of her own, but I've wondered about that, Robin. Presumably, she depended on Willie to collect people around them, and no one more capable of that than he, I imagine. He must have had loads of friends and acquaintances. Didn't she keep up with any of them?'

'Apparently not. According to Joyce Harman, she saw almost no one after he died and she suffered such agonies of shyness at parties that she nearly always turned down such invitations as did come her way. Presumably, after a month or two people just stopped asking her. That's borne out by the engagement diary, which is a positive desert from the social point of view. And it wasn't because she didn't bother to write things down. In fact, she seems to have been ultra-meticulous in that way. All her accounts and business affairs were in immaculate order and there are various entries in the diary about appointments with doctors and hairdressers, as well as reminders about paying the gas bill and so forth.'

'Doctors?'

'Yes, why not? She didn't die from an overdose, let me remind you, and I gather the post mortem showed her to be perfectly sound in wind and limb, apart from the unfortunate dent in her skull.'

'All the more surprising, I should have thought, that she should have been making appointments with doctors.'

'No, not in the least. There could be a mass of reasons. Something to do with her insurance policy, for instance, or buying an annuity. Or maybe just a routine check-up after that bout of laryngitis she had a few weeks ago.'

'Oh, yes? I should have expected a doctor to be the last man on earth she'd have wished to consult about that, but you may be right. You don't happen to know his name, by any chance?'

'No, of course not. This is not my case. The only reason for being as well informed as I am is that I knew you'd be pestering me for news the minute I arrived and I made it my business to collect a few of the answers.'

'Thank you, I do appreciate it, although it sounds pretty much like stalemate to me. Nothing to be seen but a blank wall.'

'In a way. Unless and until they find the weapon, that is.'

'Oh yes, that old sledgehammer!'

'It's such an odd feature it has put this outside the usual run of such cases. As I told you, nothing points to its being a planned murder, or indeed that murder of any kind was ever intended, so what did he use and why did he then go to such pains to conceal it?'

'How about a garden tool? I suppose they checked all those?'

'No garden. There was the usual sort of

household tool kit in one of the kitchen cupboards. Hammer, pliers and oddments of that kind, but nothing remotely the right size and weight. And in any case, why bother? Why not have just picked up a heavy saucepan, for instance, and knocked her cold with that? There was a whole battery of that iron-based enamel kind on a shelf beside the stove where she was standing. If she'd been just stunned and later recovered, so much the better, one would have thought. It would still have given him time to get as far as the other side of London before she raised the alarm, and no awkward weapon to dispose of.'

'I suppose one reason could have been that he was afraid of leaving anything behind which could give a clue to his identity. I'm not talking about finger prints, every child would know what safeguards to take there, but isn't it true that forensic medicine is so far advanced now that no criminal is proof against it? I read the other day that a tiny thread of wool, so small you could hardly see it, had eventually been matched up with a jacket belonging to one of the suspects.'

'Yes, that can happen, but . . . .'

'It would indicate that what we have here is someone rather more thoughtful and sophisticated than the average neighbourhood rapist? Is that what you were going to say?'

'Something like that.'

'Which would come as no surprise to me.'

'No, of course not, you having held the view all along that Gwen's murder was planned in advance and was part of a grand scheme involving two other deaths as well.'

'That's right!'

'Although I daresay you are no nearer to telling us who might have been the mastermind behind this operation?'

'Curiously enough, Robin, and thanks largely to Mrs Parkes, I believe I may be just half a step nearer.'

15

The church, whose interior resembled a large and magnificent eighteenth-century drawing room, which as an afterthought had been provided with altar, pulpit and pews, was three quarters full when we arrived, and once again we found places in a half empty pew at the back. This time, however, it was from necessity, not choice, for Joyce had thwarted my plan to mingle with the principal mourners and celebrants by twice going back into the house for something she had forgotten at the very point when we were about to move off. As a result, we were just able to scuttle in thirty seconds ahead of the officiating clergy.

For once, her procrastination had really exasperated me and the only consolation was that at least she was not wearing a cow pat on her head.

I did not have to dwell on these unkind

thoughts for long though, as the service lasted barely half an hour. Nigel Banks gave the address, including two anecdotes about the departed which, although singularly unfunny in my opinion, sent a dutiful ripple of amusement and appreciation round the church, and the lesson was read by James Temple/Ormsby.

This, as we could see from our card, came from the *Book of Revelations,* but ironically enough provided insight neither into the passage itself, nor into the personality of the reader. Like other writers I had listened to, he had failed to master the trick of pitching his voice up, so as to be audible from a distance of more than three feet. All the same, from one point of view, it was not a complete waste of time, because by carefully monitoring his return journey to a place on the aisle in the third row, I realised that the couple sitting next to him, who up to then had been part of the general blur, were in fact Ritchie and Helena Anstruther.

When it was over Joyce struck out on another round of dithering, searching under the hassock for her gloves and folding and re-folding the programme, so that it would fit into her bag, which she then had to open up again, to make sure her keys were inside. However, my sang froid did not desert me in this crisis, for she had provided me with the opportunity to say:

'I hope you're not in a hurry to get home? I thought we might pretend to be tourists and have lunch at one of those quaint and colourful bistros in Covent Garden.'

'Oh well, if you think so . . . I mean, thank you, that sounds very nice . . . I'd like to, only I do insist . . . I mean, I couldn't possibly let you . . . .'

'Okay, we'll go dutch, if that's what you want. In fact, we might even make it double dutch. I see Myrtle's niece Helena and her husband are here. I expect you know them don't you? They're talking to Nigel Banks at the moment, but I thought we might waylay them when they come out and invite them to join us.'

I was not sure whether she had heard me, for she had now been overtaken by a new burst of agitation and was scrabbling through her bag yet again:

'Oh yes, what a nice idea! Perhaps I'd better just check in my diary, though. My memory's getting so . . . Let's see, this is Thursday, isn't it? Oh, help! How could I

have forgotten that? No, I'm so sorry . . .
I'm afraid I can't manage . . . I've promised
a friend to go with her to the vet, to have
her beloved old cat put down. She's in such
a state . . . couldn't face it on her own, so I
said . . . Oh dear, what a pity . . . she's
coming at two o'clock.'

It was such an original excuse, brooking
no argument at all, that I made a mental
note of it, as one which might come in
handy in the future.

'Don't worry,' I told her, 'it's not important. In fact, if we make a dash for it, we
can get away without their seeing us and
avoid all the chat.'

'You mustn't think of driving me home,
you know,' she went on, panting after me
down the flight of steps to the ornamental
garden beside the church. 'No reason to
drag you away. I'll just walk through to St
Martin's Lane and get a bus.'

'You might have to wait for ages and you
mustn't be late for your friend. Besides,' I
added when we were on level ground, 'there
are a couple of things I particularly want to
ask you.'

Joyce did not look very happy to hear this
and tramped along beside me with a set

expression on her face and not uttering a word.

The silence continued until we had fought our way, yard by yard, through the lunch hour traffic round Trafalgar Square and emerged into The Mall, when I said:

'I had lunch with Eric Ingles yesterday. You remember him? The television man?'

'Oh yes, yes, indeed. A nice young man, so clever and kind. How is he?'

'Not very happy.'

'Oh dear, I'm so sorry . . . What's the trouble?'

'It seems that the play has been shelved indefinitely. He has a hunch that it's due to be buried and forgotten and that he has wasted three months of his life, not to mention heart, soul and mind, on something the viewers will never see. The annoying thing is that the people at the top are being very cagey about it and he can't find out whose spanner has screwed up the works.'

Joyce's attention had evidently been caught by something going on in St James's Park, for she had turned her head away and was staring out of the window. Speaking sternly, to recall her to business, I said:

'I daresay you would know who is responsible for this edict?'

The method worked and, jerking her head round, she replied, as it seemed, quite spontaneously for once:

'Oh well, since you ask, you are.'

'Is that so? With a little help from yourself, I take it?'

She sighed: 'There wouldn't have been any use in denying it, would there? You'd already guessed, I could tell, and you're right, of course.'

'How did you work it?'

'I got the solicitors to intervene. In my capacity as literary executor, you know. I pretended that after Gwen . . . died, when I was clearing everything up, you know, personal belongings . . . I'd come across the typescript of a novel, hidden away in a drawer in her bedroom and that I was a bit worried about some resemblances . . . Well, I needn't go into it all, need I? You can imagine the rest and I didn't mention you, or anyone else, by name. I just let them think it had come as a great shock to me.'

'And they lapped it up? Congratulations!'

'Well, I hoped you'd agree it was the right thing to do. I'd been so worried, you see, by what you'd told me about that script not being her own original work, but something of Willie's which she'd kept back and which should rightly have gone to the archives.'

'Didn't you ever get the chance to sort it out with her?'

'I did try once. I put it off for as long as I could because I hated to spoil things for her. She had so little left to live for, or look forward to, and so few resources of her own, and she was quite excited about this. But at the back of my mind I knew that arguments like that wouldn't be enough to make you drop it. You'd go on at me until I did face her with it, and there was something else you'd hinted, which made me even more afraid for her.'

'What was that?'

'When you said there might be others . . . scripts, perhaps even novels, which she'd hung on to and meant to use, if she succeeded with the first one. I could see what terrible trouble that might land her in, so in the end, just about two days before she was killed I think it was, I plucked up courage to question her about it.'

'And what was her reaction?'

'She denied it . . . Well, that is, she tried

to, but it didn't quite come off. She was sort of mutinous. She could be, you know, and she swore she had no idea what I was talking about. It was very wicked of me to make such vile threats to someone who was supposed to be a friend. Well, that didn't really hang together, if you see what I mean, and also she looked so scared, which was the worst of all. I felt sure you'd been right and I really began to wish I'd never . . . .'

'Set eyes on me?'

'No, no, I mustn't say that . . . No, of course not. It wasn't your fault and anyway, sooner or later, someone . . . . In a way, it's a relief to be able to talk openly about it, after wrestling with myself so long, and it was really me I felt vexed with. I wish now I hadn't been so ready to accept Gwen's word that she'd written the beastly thing herself. I ought to have known from the start, and in my heart of hearts I suppose I did, that it really wasn't possible.'

'And you still went ahead and got the play withdrawn, when she was dead and the danger of a repetition no longer existed. Why was that?'

'That's a bit difficult to explain,' Joyce replied.

211

Knowing her limitations in this field, I had guessed that it would be, but since we had now been swept up into the Hyde Park Corner whirligig, I was quite glad to give her a few minutes to work it out.

She used them to some purpose and, by the time we had taken the left turn into the Park, was ready to go:

'I think it was mainly because when she was dead she couldn't any longer enjoy the honour and glory and she certainly didn't need the money, so it seemed better to repair any damage that might have already been done. To let it all die away as though it had never happened, if you understand?'

'Yes, I think I do.'

'That was the main reason, but it wasn't the only one.'

'No?'

'I expect you'll think this is sentimental and silly, but it seemed to me that she wasn't in her right mind when she set off on that particular course. I don't mean she'd gone mad or anything, but, you know, not really her true self. She missed Willie so badly and her life had fallen to pieces and it made her act out of character. I do mean that quite sincerely, Miss Crichton. She may not have been a particularly lovable person and she never found it easy to get on with people, except perhaps that hairdresser and his wife she used to spend evenings with sometimes, when Willie was off somewhere on his own. But she never seemed to fit in with the sort of people Willie liked. Half the time she didn't know whether they were joking or being serious; but she wasn't really a cheat and a liar, or anything like that, and I felt sure she'd come to regret what she'd done when she was back to normal again. So, as she didn't get the chance to wipe the slate clean herself, I had this idea that it was up to me to do it for her, if you see what I mean. I expect you think I'm cracked?'

'On the contrary. None of it will do me much good, or poor Eric either, and Crispin will probably get his gun out and start shooting the cats and Charlotte as well, but from a detached point of view I am sure you did the right thing.'

'Well, that's good to hear and I'm awfully glad. Oh look, Notting Hill already! We have been quick. I'll have loads of time, so you can set me down here, if you like.'

'No, I can't. The lights will change at any

second and all forty bus drivers lined up behind us will go berserk. I'll take you to your door. It's just as easy and besides, there's still something I want to ask you.'

'Oh dear, is there really? I'm sure I can't imagine what else I . . . .'

'I just wondered why you were in such a tearing hurry to get away from the church? No business of mine, of course, but was it because I'd told you that Ritchie and Helena were there and you were trying to avoid them?'

'Ritchie and . . .' Joyce repeated in a vague voice, and then, after a pause, 'oh yes, Helena . . . you mean Myrtle's niece? I'd forgotten for the moment that her husband was called Ritchie. Such an odd name for someone who's always supposed to have been so hard up.'

'But you do know them?'

'I used to. Well, that is, I never actually met him, but I used to see a good deal of Helena at one time, before Myrtle and Willie split up. Always hanging around and on the cadge, if you really want to know. After the divorce she dropped Myrtle like a ton of bricks and switched her allegiance to Gwen.'

'To Gwen? Are you sure about that?'

'Well, tried to, I should have said. She was all over Gwen when Willie first took up with her, but she didn't make much headway. Poor Gwen was scared stiff of her and she never got it straight with Willie either.'

'Got what straight?'

'Oh dear, there I go again, putting things badly. What I meant was that for a time he used to encourage her. He'd be ready to listen to her talking about herself for hours on end. He really did listen too. Sometimes I felt I ought to warn her. Well, I was typing his book, you see, so I knew what he was up to. There was a character in it just like Helena, only much more exaggerated, as they have to be in books, you know. He really lampooned her. It was very amusing, but awfully unkind. That was the kind of heartless thing he used to do sometimes.'

'All the same, you don't sound terribly distressed about it, so perhaps I was right in thinking you didn't want to meet her today?'

'Yes, I'm afraid so . . . Well, no, not afraid at all really. I don't feel a bit guilty about not liking her and not wanting to hear her going on about what a wonderful person Myrtle was and how much she's going to miss her. But you know how childish and sort of neurotic I am about telling untruths and I do feel ashamed of myself for pretending that my friend was bringing her cat round at two o'clock, especially when it led to your driving me all the way home like this, so I shouldn't be late. The fact is, her appointment with the vet isn't till three, so I knew jolly well that I had plenty of time to get back here and have lunch as well. I'm very sorry to have deceived you and I'm sure you must think me a perfect fool, as well as a liar.'

'Nothing to feel sorry about. We've had a most interesting talk and I wouldn't have missed it for anything, but it seems to me that your dislike of Helena must go very deep for you to have gone to such lengths to avoid her, especially on an occasion like this.'

Confession had obviously improved Joyce's spirits, as well as her soul, for she replied cheerfully and with more fluency than she usually achieved:

'Well, no, I wouldn't say it did. I don't hate her, she's not worth it. I suppose despise is really the word. I haven't set eyes on her for donkey's years, but I don't suppose she's changed much and I never could stand all that affectation and showing off. She'll be worse than ever now.'

'Why's that?'

'Well, Myrtle was quite well off, you know. Very well off, by my standards.'

'Was she? What's that got to do with. . . .'

'Oh yes, very well off. You mustn't think she lived in that funny old basement because she couldn't afford anything better. That was the kind of background that suited her. She had no use for possessions and she was bone lazy about domestic chores. All except cooking, of course, she loved that. But she had a good settlement from Willie and she made an absolute packet out of her books for about fifteen years. I doubt if she spent a quarter of her income.'

We had arrived outside Joyce's front door by this time and I pulled on the handbrake, saying:

'Well, that's all very fascinating, but I still don't understand how it's going to make Helena show off more than ever. Perhaps you could spell it out for me?'

'Oh, didn't I explain? There now, what a mutt I am! Helena was her sole heir. She was Myrtle's next of kin and the will was drawn up ages ago, when she was married to Willie and Helena couldn't do enough for her. I don't know why she never bothered to change it. She wasn't vindictive, of course, and I daresay she just kept putting it off. She probably felt there'd be oceans of time to do it one day, when she felt in the mood for it. She had such a zest for life, poor Myrtle, and I don't suppose it entered her head that one of those heart attacks could carry her off.'

'And it's a lot of money, you say?'

'Well, you know, I couldn't tell you exactly, but . . . that is, yes, really quite a lot of money. So there'll be no holding that two-faced Helena now. I expect the first thing she'll do is get rid of the dingy little house in Blackheath she was always moaning about and splash out on a grand new one. Well, thank you very much. I'm sorry to have been such a pest.'

She was fumbling, in her usual uncoordinated fashion, with the door handle, so I stretched across and raised it for her, saying as I did so:

'Myrtle may have thought she had all the time in the world, but evidently Helena was under no such illusion.'

'Oh, why? Why do you say that?'

'You've been out of touch with her, so this will come as news to you, but she's done it already. She's got rid of the dingy little house in Blackheath and splashed out on a grand new one.'

16

So many interesting facts had come to light during this journey through London that it was not until I was bowling back along the Bayswater Road that I realised that there was one question which I had forgotten to ask Joyce. This oversight was interesting too in its way, because during the inaudible stretches of the service, when my mind had wandered free, it had loomed as among the most important. However, I had found that such lapses are not always attributable to forgetfulness alone. Instinct can play a part and can often be right. In view of the ramifications which every new encounter seemed to bring, I decided that it had probably been right this time and that for the moment I should wade no further into these waters, but appeal to Robin for the answer to my last question.

I began by explaining: 'Please understand

that I am not taking this seriously. My theory is purely hypothetical and has been worked out for my own amusement, but it is rather like a crossword puzzle. Having filled in one and five across and two down and now discovered a fourth word, which would link them all up, I can't bear to leave that corner unfinished.'

'What are the first three words?' he asked.

'Willie, Myrtle and Gwen. I do realise that two of them died from natural causes, but Gwen most certainly did not, and since Willie was married to both the others, it is logical to start with those three.'

'If you say so. What's your fourth word?'

'That's Helena. You must admit she fits. The possibility hadn't struck me until today, but as soon as Joyce told me that Helena used to haunt the house in South Park Terrace, when Myrtle was the queen bee, and did her damnedest to go on haunting it after the crown had passed to Gwen and that, for reasons of his own, Willie encouraged her, I saw what a heavy link in the chain she could turn out to be.'

'So what is it you want me to do?'

'Just a small matter of checking on yet another name. I did mention this once before, but it was only a passing thought then. I'd like you to find out who was Gwen's doctor, the one she had an appointment with just before she was killed.'

'Oh well, I suppose that might be managed without too much difficulty.'

'I hope so because, if I've guessed right, it gives me seven across as well and makes a neat job of it.'

'And that will finish it off for you, will it?'

'It will finish the top left hand corner. I can't tell yet, but if that comes off I might just have a go at the right hand one. Only as an exercise, you understand? I don't want to get rusty.'

'Quite honestly, I wouldn't mind how rusty you got, but I don't expect that to carry any weight. Are you also likely to need assistance from me with the right hand corner?'

'Since you so kindly offer, there could be one small point you could check for me. I expect Joyce has got her facts right. I'm beginning to believe that she invariably does and that Myrtle knew what she was talking about when she described her as a formidable old party. I can't make out whether her diffidence is partly an act, or whether she really did acquire an incurable inferiority complex from that bully of a headmistress. Anyway, there's no harm in double checking.'

'Do you want me to get a report from her psychiatrist, by any chance?'

'Oh no, all that was just by the way. What I need to be sure about are the terms of Myrtle's will and I'd also like to know how much she left. Joyce says there would have been quite a whack and that Helena gets the lot, but she's rather unworldly and quite a lot to her might mean a couple of thousand to the rest of us. Could you find out for me?'

'Yes, I can see how that would get you off to a good start. And that's really all, is it?'

'For the moment yes, thank you, darling. If I remember anything else before you leave for work tomorrow, I'll let you know. It would be a pity not to make the most of this co-operative mood while it lasts. None of the usual cautions, I notice, about staying out of trouble and minding my own business?'

'That's partly because you say you're only doing this for fun.'

'Partly?'

'Why, yes. The main reason, if you'll forgive my saying so, is that it doesn't seem to me that anything you've asked for could possibly have the slightest bearing on Gwen's murder. So I don't see what possible harm it could do to you, or anyone else, to carry on with the game.'

It was the second time he had administered this patronising, metaphorical pat on the head and the temptation to strike him was not made easier to resist by the knowledge that he was most likely right.

Fortunately for my amour propre, I had something to read which was specifically designed to take my mind off the current state of frustration and stalemate. This was the pilot script for a six-part television serial, which, after much nagging and several weeks' delay, I had at last prevailed on my agent to send me.

'I can't think why you're so keen,' she had grumbled. 'It's not a part for you at all. This character is supposed to be about sixty. She has to be about sixty, otherwise it wouldn't make sense, and she has all the lines. The romantic leads are just nothing.'

'Never mind, I'd still like to read it, if it's

not putting you to too much trouble.'

'It definitely is putting me to too much trouble. It's a waste of time and I'm not even sure that I've still got it.'

'Yes, you have. You told me yourself that you hadn't sent it back and, God knows, nothing in your office ever gets thrown away. Just tell one of your minions to spend the morning turning the place upside down until she finds it.'

It had arrived in the post the day after my inconclusive wrangle with Robin, and as soon as he had left for work I told Mrs Cheeseman that I had business to do which could best be done propped up in bed and did not wish to be disturbed, except in cases of emergency. As she regularly punctuates her morning toil with at least three emergencies, I considered that the normal quota would provide as much disturbance as I could take in my stride.

Predictably enough, it was a murder mystery, and like many first ventures into the medium of television drama, was partly autobiographical, as I could vouch for, having met the auto whose biography it was based on.

The protagonist was an elderly but intrepid woman named Mamie Spinks, writer of children's books and spare time amateur detective. However, this was no sweet little old lady stereotype, spending her days listening to village gossip and knitting mysterious garments which never got finished. Mamie was an extrovert of forceful character and sharp intelligence, who blew through everyone's life with the speed of a gale force wind, overturning every apple cart that lay in her path, and I could see why Aurora Withers had been attracted to the idea of playing her. For one thing, as my agent had warned me, she had all the good lines and there were plenty of those; whereas, with two exceptions, the subsidiary characters were shadowy almost to the point of non-existence. The main function of all of them, including the young couple, whose landlord and persecutor it was who had been murdered, appeared to be to provide Mamie with the cue for her next witticism.

The two exceptions were a pushy, go-getting and philandering young man named Jack, who was Mamie's stepson, left over from one of several marriages and also a potential suspect, in that he was heavily in debt to the landlord and also deceiving his stuck-up girl friend, Harriet, by having an affair with the landlord's wife.

The second character to have been more than perfunctorily sketched in was one called Janet, Mamie's illustrator and adoring friend. Although reputed to be a talented artist, she was a dowdy, subservient sort of woman, thoroughly cowed by the whirlwind Mamie. However, she had a touch or two of reality about her, a suggestion of hidden depths and a hint or two that, as the plot developed, Janet would be the one to keep an eye on.

The closing scene of this first episode, in my opinion, was neither convincing nor sufficiently suspenseful, but apart from this and one or two other minor flaws, most of which could easily be put right on the studio floor, it was well above the average for this type of light entertainment. I awarded my agent low marks for having allowed it to moulder, unnoticed and unsung, for all these months in her office.

However, my chief interest in this script lay not in its merits, but in comparing it with the one whose every line I could have recited from memory and which was now mouldering in the office of Eric Ingles. In that sense, it had been a profitable exercise, since it had removed the last lingering doubt that they both came from the same pen. Clearly, Myrtle's technique had improved by several strides during the interval which separated them, but there were enough similarities, notably in the phrasing and rhythm of the dialogue, to rule out any alternative.

This was satisfactory, as far as it went, but on the debit side, as Robin would have pointed out with the speed and smugness of a darts player hitting the board squarely on target, the solution to Gwen's murder remained as elusive as ever.

The morning had also produced its average crop of emergencies, including, most recently, the news that I should not be able to have my bath until goodness knew when, every tap in the house having run dry, owing to a burst water main on the other side of the square. Being resigned to spending the rest of my life in bed, sooner than face the world without a hot bath, I plunged back on to the pillows for a second reading of the Myrtle Sprygge television script, Mark 1.

Before I had got through the first ten pages a small light had begun to cast its glow over the darker patches of my mind and I raced through the next twenty, paying special attention to the names of all the main characters and checking off each indication that I was on the right lines as I came to it.

The last two pages were still unread when the water began gurgling through the pipes again and Mrs Cheeseman's tune had changed to a lament about the chances of getting this bedroom tidied up before lunch, but I no longer cared. I had read enough for my purpose and had by then brought my intellectual powers to bear on an article in a woman's magazine, telling us how to create sculptures out of ice. It did not inspire me, for it seemed to require an immense amount of fiddling about for such an evanescent kind of end product. It was simply a case of filling in time until the moment arrived for Robin to throw out his next little taunt about nothing I had achieved so far having brought me any nearer to discovering who had murdered Gwen Montgomerie.

Less than eight hours later he gave me just the cue I needed, but I let it go by, preferring to wait until I had collected whatever crumbs he might be about to scatter, before moving down for the curtain line.

I had begun by asking: 'Were you able to find out anything about the terms of Myrtle's will?'

'Yes, and your lucky star was really burning brightly for you that time because the will hasn't been filed yet and there's just no other way I could have found out what was in it.'

'So how did you manage it?'

'She and Gwen were both looked after by Willie's family solicitors. One of the partners is also Gwen's executor and so, as you can imagine, my obliging colleague, who shall be nameless, for fear of his being drummed out of the force for breach of confidence, has been having a number of consultations with him.'

'Oh yes, that is good news. And he actually threw in something about Myrtle's will too?'

'Purely off the cuff. It came up when he was talking about how little Willie had been able to leave Gwen to live on and how comparatively much better off than either of them his first wife had been. Never one to turn down the chance to acquire some extra circumstantial evidence, however remote, my colleague expressed a polite interest and learnt that, in fact, your informant was right.'

'Good old Joyce! Any details?'

'It was quite straightforward. Apart from some minor bequests, including five hundred pounds and a ruby brooch to Miss Harman herself incidentally, the whole lot goes to Myrtle's niece, Helena Anstruther.'

'And is it what they call a tidy sum?'

'It is very what I call tidy. Over two hundred thousand, before tax.'

'Oh, my goodness, as much as that? No wonder Helena has such a guilty conscience about neglecting poor old auntie in her declining years.'

'Although I understand she did nothing of the kind. Didn't Ritchie tell you that, in fact, she was most attentive and made a point of visiting Myrtle at least once a month?'

'Yes, he did and I see it all now. At first I thought he simply said it because he's conditioned to perpetuating the myth that Helena's such a saint. That's obviously how she wants the world to see her, and obviously too she is much easier to live with if there are plenty of worshippers at the shrine. Therefore, Ritchie, who is either brainwashed, or scared to death of her, goes around making sure the supply doesn't run out. That was my analysis at the time, but now I begin to realise that there was most likely more than a grain of truth in what he told me.'

'Why's that?'

'Because the news about Myrtle's will changes everything. One can be fairly certain Helena knew she stood to inherit everything, so long as Myrtle didn't change her mind, so she wouldn't have been the one to bring that about. She no longer bothered to invite Myrtle to the house because she was getting old and eccentric and, more to the point, no longer a celebrity to be shown off to the elite of Blackheath. But she was still a valuable property in the other sense and I don't doubt that Helena took care to keep in touch with her and occasionally spend a few hours in the despised little Swiss Cottage flat. So I am now striking a balance between the two versions by assuming that Ritchie exaggerated Helena's dutiful devotion by exactly the same proportion as

Helena underplayed it.'

'In which case,' Robin said, in the now familiar bantering tone of a schoolmaster putting down a bumptious pupil, 'if only it were Myrtle's death which was under investigation, you could consider yourself home and dry. However, at the risk of being a bore, I must remind you once again that it is not Myrtle who has been killed, but Gwen.'

'Oh, I know, I know, and I'm not bothered about that for the moment. All I wanted was to make sure Joyce had got her facts right.'

'And now that you have, what difference does it make?'

'None at all, I daresay, but she is my only source of information and the only person, apart from Willie, and possibly her hairdresser, whom Gwen appears to have confided in. So long as I'm playing my crossword game, it's as well to know how much reliance I can put on what she tells me. She is, after all, the only surviving member of that triple alliance, so it would be stupid not to prise as much as I can out of her, before she gets knocked off too.'

'What triple alliance?'

233

'Willie, Myrtle and Joyce, the three people who, between them, made up the back, middle and foreground of Gwen's life. Apart from them, it seems to have been singularly underpopulated and that's precisely why, whether you agree or not, I still feel that the more I learn about them the more will be revealed about Gwen. It is only a game, as I've told you.'

'Yes, and I must try to remember. Sometimes, listening to you, it is almost possible to believe that you are beginning to take it seriously.'

'Oh, that is the way to play games,' I assured him. 'It is only the serious things one can afford to be flippant about. Games are like farce in the theatre. By the way, Robin, were you able to find out the answer to the other question I gave you?'

'Can't remember. What was it?'

'The name of Gwen's doctor.'

'Oh yes, that's right, yes, I did. His name is Carter.'

'Carter? Are you sure?'

'Of course I'm sure. My sources are unlikely to have got it wrong.'

'Well, that's most disappointing, I must say, and bang goes seven across. Where have

I slipped up and why do you start reading the evening paper when we're in the middle of a conversation?'

'Are we in the middle of a conversation? I thought we'd finished it.'

'Did you honestly, Robin?'

'No.'

'Oh, I see! You mean there's still something you have to tell me, but you don't want me to know what it is?'

'I hadn't made up my mind. I had my own private idea of what seven across was all about and when I heard this fellow's name was Carter I felt relieved. Well, that's that, I thought. False trail, full stop. Unfortunately, though, it didn't end there and my over-zealous colleague had to go and fill in the background, as well.'

'Which was?'

'Well, I suppose it would be petty to deny you your small triumph. Carter, who is Australian, was taken on a few years ago, as junior partner, by a man already established in Harley Street. He has now more or less taken over the practice, except for a very few old patients, who did not, I must emphasise, did not include Gwen.'

'The name of the senior partner being

Dr James Temple?'

'Otherwise, I wouldn't have made this futile attempt to keep it dark, would I? I can't imagine why I bothered. You'd have got it out of me sooner or later, and after all, what can it matter? It was a lucky guess and you're entitled to know that you were right, as far as it went, but it has no other bearing, as far as I can see. Gwen was Carter's patient, not Temple's, and furthermore, as I repeat ad nauseam, she did not die from an overdose, or some illness which required a doctor's certificate. There is nothing whatever to connect either Carter or Temple with her murder.'

'Not so far,' I replied, picking up my cue this time.

'And what is that inscrutable remark meant to convey?'

'Just that nothing you've told me may be important, but it still doesn't induce me to give up my crossword. I've just discovered, you see, that James Temple turns up in another context in another part of the puzzle. Only in that clue he's presented as Jack.'

17

The following morning I was mooning round Hatchards, having called there to collect a book Toby wanted me to take down to Roakes with me that afternoon, when I saw a man, a few yards away from me, behaving like a shoplifter. Statistics prove that I am surrounded by such people every time I enter a shop and, indeed, am liable at any moment to discover that I have joined their ranks, but this was the first time I had seen one in action.

He had stationed himself in the angle formed by a wall and the end of a long shelf against the window and was thus protected from the passing throng. Nevertheless, after observing him carefully for a few minutes, in the interests of my art, I became mystified, not only by his methods, but by the fact that they had not already drawn him to the notice of the store detective.

He was wearing a heavy, country-style waterproof coat, with flaps and pockets galore and a brown trilby hat, all of which should have been a dead giveaway, and appeared to be re-arranging a pile of books, which he then exchanged for a similar pile nearer the centre of the shelf. The operation was furtively but deftly accomplished and I could not but admire the sleight of hand, whereby he had presumably transferred one or more of the original pile into a pocket. Having completed the business, he stood back to appraise the effect, then turned and, in the same instant, saw me watching him.

It was curious because, up till then, he was someone whose range of facial expressions I had believed to be limited to those of an indignant fox and a fox in a fury. In this crisis, he contrived to look indignant, sheepish, furious and embarrassed all at the same time.

Taking embarrassment to be paramount in this turmoil of emotions and feeling sorry for him, as a result, I fell into a familiar patter. I did not actually say: 'Darling, you were marvellous!' but modified it to:

'I've been hanging around, trying to screw up my courage to accost you and say how very much I admired your address at the memorial service. It was so moving and yet so funny, too.'

'Thanks. Good of you to say so. You were there, were you? Well, must have been, of course.'

'Yes and I found it all most impressive. And so beautifully organised. I expect you were responsible for that, too?'

'Oh Lord, no, nothing to do with me. Well, perhaps a few suggestions here and there. Went all right, did it?'

'Oh, absolutely!' I replied, unprepared for his being as insatiable as the actor in his dressing room and beginning to run out of superlatives.

'Good! Time for a drink, or do you have business to do here?'

'No, I've finished now and I'd love a drink. How very kind of you!'

'I feel this must be a unique occasion,' I remarked, when he had conducted me to the basement bar of a raffish old pub in the hinterland of Jermyn Street and set us up with a glass of wine and a large scotch.

'Oh, really? Why's that?'

'It must be the first time I've ever cashed

in a rain check. It's a phrase which people use all the time, but it's become as meaning-less as "when are you coming to see us" or "we must have lunch." '

'Yes, stupid expression, really. Cheers!'

'It's nice and quiet down here. Do you come often?'

'Used to. Not so much now.'

It was uphill work and I was not making much headway with my cocktail party small talk, so deciding I had nothing to lose by introducing the subject that weighed most heavily, I said:

'I hope you won't mind my asking, but I've been wondering what you were doing just now with that pile of books. I thought at first, before I recognised you, that you were a shoplifter, but that didn't quite fit and certainly not in your case. I mean, why would a writer want to steal someone else's books? It would be like a farmer stealing his neighbour's apples.'

Mr Banks gave a fox-like bark, which was presumably the nearest he could get to laughter, and then turned sheepish again:

'They weren't someone else's books, they were mine.'

'You can't be serious? Surely, you get all

the free copies you want? Why should you need to pinch them?'

'I wasn't pinching them. Just . . . well, tidying them up, you might say.'

'Oh, I see!'

'No, you don't. And stop looking at me as though I ought to be in a strait jacket. Better you should learn the sordid truth than go away with the idea that I'm raving mad. I don't know though,' he muttered, staring moodily into his glass, 'perhaps if I do tell you it won't change your mind and you may be right. Perhaps I am a bit mad. I often wonder about it.'

'You were just tidying up,' I prompted.

'Right! I've got a new book just out, you see.'

'Congratulations! What's it called?'

'Come to that in a minute. To get back to the point, I happened to be in Piccadilly this morning on my way to lunch, and I had some time to fill in, so I thought I might as well just stop by that place and make sure they'd got their socks pulled up. Have to watch these booksellers, you know. Sloppy lot, some of them.'

'Yes, I'm sure. How were their socks this morning?'

'Not too bad. They'd got three or four copies quite well displayed in the window, which was all right, so then I thought, as I was there, I might as well take a look inside.'

'And what did you find?'

'Chaos. First thing was, I couldn't see a single copy on that stand by the window, where they ought to have been. Then, when I'd poked around a bit, I found they'd got half a dozen of them stacked up at the end of the shelf, where you could hardly get near them. To crown it all, some careless ass had stuck a completely different novel on top of the pile. So the first thing was to get rid of that.'

'And then move the rest to a more advantageous position? Yes, I quite understand.'

'And no doubt writing me off as an egomaniac already half way round the bend?'

'Not at all. I often go through the same sort of ritual with the box office.'

'Do you now? I'm surprised to hear that. Far as I can make out, when some new play comes on, however rubbishy, all the papers carry reviews the next morning. Not necessarily flattering reviews, but at least the public knows all about it

242

and where to find it.'

'Yes, we do score in that way, I agree, but it doesn't always end there, you know. Socks can slip at the box office too. Not everyone leaps to answer the telephone on the first ring, and apart from that, there's a sort of compulsion to check on the takings for each performance. So I'm all on your side you see, and next time I'm in a bookshop I'll make it my business to see they're on their toes and everything of yours is properly displayed.'

This effusiveness was not wholly insincere, for the discovery that he did, after all, belong to the human race, with all its frailties, including raving egomania, had quite endeared him to me and I had spun out my drink, to give him the excuse to order another for himself, which he seemed quite eager to do.

'And now, I suppose, you are on your way to be fêted at a celebration lunch with your publishers?' I enquired, when he returned with the second large scotch.

'No, that was yesterday. They laid on a do for the press and what not. Today I'm taking Joyce out to lunch. Always need to fortify myself for that.'

'Joyce?'

'Harman. Remember her, do you? You met at Myrtle's funeral.'

'Oh yes, and once or twice since then. Is she an old friend of yours?'

'You could say that, I suppose. I've known her a good many years.'

'So why do you need to be fortified to take her out to lunch?'

'Ah well, she does go rambling on a bit, you know. Makes it hard to keep in step sometimes. I daresay you found the same? She told me you gave her a lift back into London that time, after the funeral.'

'Yes, I find her conversation a trifle disjointed, but I put it down to shyness. There doesn't seem to be much wrong with her brain. Quite sharp, in fact.'

'Oh, you bet, sharp as a needle. Observant too, in her funny way. She picks up things most people wouldn't notice. Trouble with Joyce, though, is that she's gone through life with blinkers on. Hasn't much awareness of what's going on in the world outside. It sometimes leads her into false conclusions.'

'Because she's never married, you mean?'

'No, I don't, not at all what I mean. I

244

haven't been married myself, come to that, but I don't consider it's given me illusions about the rest of mankind. What I meant about Joyce was that she's been protected from most of the realities in that close little world of hers. She's lived life at second hand and it sometimes affects her judgement. She's got some new bee in her bonnet now, which she wants to tell me about. It'll probably turn out to be largely imaginary and a lot of fuss about nothing, but you can never tell with Joyce. Anyway, I said we'd better discuss it over lunch. I feel sorry for her, as a matter of fact. Do her good to get out and about for a bit.'

'Sorry for her because of Gwen?'

'Not only her, all three of them. Willie and Myrtle and Gwen, too, to some extent, but Willie most of all. He was the sun who kept those three female satellites spinning around in his orbit and when he died they all seemed to disintegrate in some way. I feel sorry for Joyce because she's come off worst of all, with the other two gone now, but it was Willie's death which really knocked her out. She'd known him longest of all of them and was the most dependent. At least, those two wives of his managed to keep some part of themselves separate from him. Myrtle certainly did and even Gwen . . . well, that's another story, but Joyce was completely single-minded.'

'I wouldn't claim to know her nearly so well as you obviously do, but curiously enough, I've sometimes heard her speak in quite a detached, almost critical way about him.'

'And why not? I said she was single-minded, not simple. It was not blind hero worship, or the abject devotion of some sexually repressed spinster. Her feelings went much deeper than that. Ah well, mustn't go on gassing about it. Simply trying to explain why I feel a kind of obligation to try and prop her up a bit during this rough patch. Come on, drink up if you want another! If you've time, that is?'

I should have liked nothing better than another and would willingly have sacrificed my hairdressing appointment to make time for it, for he had made a number of remarks, and one in particular, which I would have dearly liked to follow up. However, I considered it more politic to leave Mr Banks with the impression that my pleasure in conversing with him had been a tribute to his charm, rather than any special interest in the subject. So I said goodbye, wished him success with the book and repeated my promise to cast an eye over the display counter when I bought my own copy. As an afterthought, I added that I hoped he would call on us one evening and autograph it for me.

The combined effects of double whiskies and double doses of flattery had turned him into a very benign fox by then and all he needed to complete the picture was a frilly nightcap.

'So there's my rain check for you,' I said, 'and don't imagine you'll be allowed to get off without cashing it.'

18

'I am not at all sure that I like it,' were Toby's first words when I arrived at Roakes Common the same evening.

'Nothing new in that. What is it you're not liking at the moment?'

'Your new hairstyle, if style is the word.'

'Is it the colour you object to?'

'Yes, the colour is rather horrid and I think all that frizz may have been a mistake too.'

'I am inclined to agree with you, but beggars can't be choosers.'

'You mean you didn't have to pay for it? Well, that's something, I suppose, although I still consider it was a false economy.'

'I don't mean anything of the kind. This was a different sort of begging. In fact, I had to pay through the nose.'

'You amaze me! Has Robin seen it yet?'

'No, I only had it done this afternoon.'

'Well, I should warn you that it is bound to be a shock, but perhaps he will get to like it, given time.'

'He won't be required to get to like it. As soon as I arrive in London on Monday I shall go straight to my regular hairdresser, and when he comes out of his faint, he will undo all the damage.'

'So you found a new man to create this wreckage for you? Rather rash, wasn't it?'

'Yes, it was, but he was the nearest one I could find of the right sort of level to number sixteen South Park Terrace, so I took a chance. Cut Above they're called, by the way, though Cut And Don't Come Again might be more in line with the Trade Descriptions Act. Anyway, when my guess turned out right, I couldn't just settle for an ordinary old wash and blow dry. It had to be something which involved the exchange of a small fortune.'

'Why was that?'

'To break down the reserves, of course. Get them all running round, showering me with biscuits and coffee and indulging my every conversational whim.'

'And it worked? That rather surprises me too. They might have taken you for a newspaper reporter.'

'Of course they took me for a newspaper reporter. I should have been mortified if they hadn't, since that's what I was passing myself off as. Well, what would you have done, Toby? I could hardly say I was a friend of Gwen's, who had recommended me to them. In that case, I should presumably have known far more about her than I was hoping to find out from them. Nor would it have been very artistic to pretend that I just happened to be passing and then, having dropped in for a three hour session, to have piped up with: "Oh yes, isn't it somewhere round here where that poor woman was attacked and murdered in her own house?" That could have led to finding myself surrounded by half a dozen pink-overalled deaf mutes.'

'Which is precisely the effect the word "reporter" is liable to have on a lot of people.'

'Only not, on the whole, on hairdressers. However much they might resent some nosey stranger, inspired by sheer, vulgar curiosity, a professional with a handsome expense account would be treated with respect. In fact, if I were a gossip columnist I should make it my business to spend part of every working day in some hairdressing establishment with an upper crust clientele and just sit back and listen.'

'So, having done so this afternoon, what did the harvest bring?'

'Practically nothing.'

'Oh, my God! Has all this build-up been just to tell me that?'

'That's the paradox. Practically nothing is exactly what I was hoping for. Nothing at all would have been no use. It would simply have meant that, despite its location and the fact that it was the rather dowdy sort of place I associate with women like Gwen, I had picked the wrong one and would have to start again from scratch. As it was, I learnt that she had been a customer, though not by any means one of their big spenders. She had a standing appointment to have her hair washed every Thursday morning and about once a month she had it cut as well. In addition, she was very polite, never made a fuss if she was kept waiting and would never consent to try a new style.'

'Unlike some!'

'Yes, well, I'm sorry you find it so objectionable, but the worst of it will brush out, and as I've explained, it was all in a good cause.'

'Though I fail to see what you have to be so pleased about, if that was your only reward.'

'Then I'll tell you, and I have to begin by explaining that judging by appearance, it's doubtful whether Joyce has ever been to a hairdresser in her life. She probably holds her head under the kitchen tap and then gives it a good rub down with a bath towel. So, presumably, it wouldn't have occurred to her that for someone who spent so much time and money on the business, Gwen had remarkably little to show for it. It's still more unlikely that Willie would ever have questioned it. After a certain number of years I doubt if many men do notice their wives' appearance very often, unless someone else draws their attention to it.'

'Then I must endeavour not to do so when Robin arrives,' Toby said.

'I am afraid that won't save me. Robin is different. For one thing, I like to think that we haven't yet been married long enough for me to have become invisible, but I also have a notion that he will still be noticing me when I am quite old. That's because he has been trained, or has trained himself, to notice everything. Even a missing ashtray can be a worry, but from all I hear, Willie was not like that at all. He was the centre of his own universe and other people only impinged on him in so far as they affected his comfort and convenience, or if he happened to be using them as models for characters in a book.'

'Enough of these abstract reflections! What does it all boil down to?'

'Simply that, for reasons heretofore touched upon, neither Willie nor Joyce would have found anything incredible in Gwen's claim to have spent so much of her time getting her hair fixed. Neither did they find anything strange about the fact that from time to time, when Willie was out on pursuits of his own, from which she was excluded, she should have elected to spend the evening with Mr and Mrs Cut Above in their flat over the shop.'

'And why not? No doubt, she found most of Willie's circle rather a strain to keep up with, and having worked in the trade herself, what more natural than that she should have found their company congenial?'

'Several things more natural, in my opinion, the chief one being that although she may not have felt entirely at home in her new surroundings, it did not prevent her striving to fit into them. She took great pride in being the wife of Willie Montgomerie, as was evident by her presence at the Alibi Club dinner. Her aim would have been to cut herself off as far as possible from the old associations with those humbler days and to leave the world of shampoos and conditioners far behind her. At least, that was my guess and I was probably right because it was quite obvious that this lot would scarcely have recognised Gwen if they'd passed her in the street, unless she happened to be wearing a hair net, and there was certainly no social hobnobbing.'

'They might not have told you if there had been.'

'Oh yes, they would. The proprietor and the staff too were agog with excitement when they discovered I was a newspaper woman. You could see the glint in their eyes, as visions swam before them of being paid a million pounds for the exclusive story called "The Gwen Montgomerie I Knew". Even at a modest reckoning, it would have been a tremendous advertising boost for the shop and they were digging up, or inventing, every detail about her that came into their heads. Not that it amounted to a row of hairpins though, and so the big question is: if Gwen didn't go round to see them on her evenings off, where did she go and who was she spending them with?'

'Don't tell me you don't know the answer!'

'Not yet, I don't, but I should think it would be fairly easy to find it, wouldn't you?'

'No.'

'Oh, please don't be so negative, Toby. It is most discouraging and I get enough of that from Robin.'

'Not quite enough, apparently, if you seriously imagine you can find an open door where the entire Metropolitan CID have spent the last couple of weeks banging their collective noses against a brick wall.'

'That's only because they don't have access to the kind of information which gets handed to me on my daily round, without my even having to ask for it.'

'I thought you told me it didn't amount to a row of hairpins?'

'Oh, I'm no longer thinking of that part

of the round. It was useful, insofar as it tied up the parcel in pink ribbon, but the contents were already inside. I got some of them from a television script, which fell into my hands the other day, some from a conversation I had in the kitchen with Mrs Parkes one Sunday morning and the rest as a result of being picked up in a bookshop. It just goes to show that it is not always unwise to accept favours from strange men. Few men could be stranger than Nigel Banks, but, as well as a drink, he gave me one very valuable tip. Don't you want me to tell you what it was?'

'Is there anything at all which would stop you?'

'It was involuntary, I think, and he slid away from it and on to something else as soon as the words were out, but it was enough to indicate that, despite what her nearest, if not dearest, may have believed, Gwen did have a side to her life which she kept secret from all three of them.'

'So all you have to do, I suppose, is to find out what, or rather who her secret was? It is difficult to see where you might start.'

'No, that has already been decided. I mean to start in Harley Street.'

'Do you indeed?'

'Thanks again, largely, to Nigel Banks, who knows a lot of people who travel through life under pseudonyms and therefore sees them in a different light from the rest of us, I think that is my best bet. An interesting, if not unique location too, don't you agree? Just two streets further down the road from the Cut Above and you could walk there from South Park Terrace in under ten minutes. So no trouble about buses or taxis, where a regular passenger, even one as dim as Gwen, might have been noticed and remembered. Another nice thing about Harley Street is that during the daytime it's so clogged from end to end with people and cars that one individual would be as hard to single out as a pebble on Brighton beach; whereas in the evenings it's a desert. I don't suppose more than a couple of dozen people actually live there and you might walk down the length of it, after six o'clock, without meeting a soul.'

'Why do you find it necessary to tell me these things? I may have led a sheltered life, but it has nevertheless included a slight acquaintance with Harley Street.'

'I am simply pointing out how easy it

would be for someone who did live there to lead another sort of sheltered life; sheltered, that is, from the prying eyes of neighbours or a policeman on the beat.'

'The one you have in mind being Dr James Temple, I take it?'

'Alias Ormsby, the science fiction writer. Correct.'

'Who, in such spare time as was left to him, was engaged in a clandestine affair with Gwen Montgomerie, until one evening, for reasons known only to himself, he broke into her house and murdered her? Perhaps she was trying to force him into marriage and he preferred his bachelor quarters above the consulting room?'

'Something on those lines,' I admitted. 'I was hoping it would turn out that he had done the murdering part on his own premises, then driven her home at dead of night and dumped her on the kitchen floor, but unfortunately Robin tells me it is out of the question. She died on the spot where she fell. I suppose it would be too much to hope that he is spending this weekend with the Anstruthers?'

'Not as far as I know. Mrs Parkes could tell you, but in any case I fail to see how it could help you very much, if he were. I seem to recall that you did not have a thumping success when you tried to engage him in conversation once before. To be fair, if you are right about him, the circumstances were against you, since it must have been very soon after he had killed his mistress, so he could well have been feeling down in the mouth, although I still consider it unlikely that he would be any more willing to confide in you now.'

'Me or anyone else, and I wouldn't be such a fool as to expect him to. All the same, when people have something to conceal they often try to blanket it by chatting away rather freely on what they believe to be an unrelated subject and that can sometimes give you a lever. However, I shall have to do the best I can with Helena.'

'Oh, surely not? What have you got against Helena, apart from what we've all got?'

'Oh, just another theory which I picked up from Myrtle's script. It might be worth following up. Besides, Robin hasn't met her yet. I'd really like his opinion, and with any luck he'll be down early tomorrow morning. Would you have any objection to my inviting them over for a drink before lunch?'

'I have every objection under the sun and much good it will do me. Oh dear, what a fearful bore! Ritchie will send us into a torpor by going on about how wonderful Helena is and Helena will sit there with a smirk on her face, using all her tedious wiles to beg, borrow or steal Mrs Parkes from me. I do wish they had never come to live here. I sometimes think that even dogs or children might have been preferable.'

19

'I hope you haven't caught the clairvoyancy bug,' Robin said, when he had recovered from the initial shock of Cut Above's handiwork. 'Do you suppose Myrtle can have used some witch's device to hand it on to you?'

'I hope not. Why do you ask?'

'Do you remember telling me the other day that you were anxious to get as much information out of Joyce as you could, before she got knocked off too?'

'That was meant to be a joke. Please don't tell me that she has been?'

'Not as bad as that, but somebody may conceivably have had that in mind and she was lucky to have come out almost unscathed.'

'Out of what?'

'Yesterday afternoon she came very close to being run over by a train at Green Park underground station.'

'Pushed on the line, you mean?'

'Not necessarily, although, as I said, there is a remote possibility of it.'

'Is she all right?'

'So far as I know. She had no serious injuries, just a few scrapes and bruises, but she was in a bad state of shock and they kept her in the hospital overnight.'

'How exactly did it happen?'

'The head of the train had just appeared in the tunnel and everyone surged forward, as they do at that point. There's a rather limited service on Saturday afternoons, so some of them had been waiting twenty minutes or more and weren't going to risk being left behind. Either through misjudgement, or for some more sinister reason, Joyce ended up with one leg over the platform and would have fallen the whole way, if someone hadn't grabbed hold and hauled her back.'

'Would she have been killed otherwise?'

'It's a moot point. The driver had noticed some kind of skirmish going on and could probably have been able to stop in time, but it must have been a nasty moment.'

'Although, presumably, since she wasn't

knocked unconscious or anything, she has a pretty good idea herself whether it was an accident, or whether someone in the crowd gave her an extra shove?'

'And thereby hangs a tale. In the ambulance she was babbling on in a rather incoherent fashion about how she travelled by tube every day of her life and nothing like this had ever happened to her before.'

'That I can believe. She is apt to be slightly incoherent, even when she is not in a state of shock.'

'Yes, but the gist of it was that it couldn't have happened unless some malicious person had engineered it.'

'And she ought to know. It is the kind of thing one would be likely to notice.'

'She ought to, but apparently she didn't because by nine o'clock this morning she had retracted every word. She was blaming the incident entirely on herself and apologising to everyone in sight for giving them so much trouble.'

'Yes, that sounds fairly typical too. Poor old thing, I must send her some flowers. On second thoughts, perhaps it would be a better idea to take them round in person.'

'Better in what way?'

'Just that, from a curiosity point of view, I wouldn't mind seeing what sort of place she lives in.'

'Nothing else in mind?'

'Well, since you ask, Robin, I would quite like to hear at first hand what really happened in the underground station. I do find that part rather strange, you know. She says some weird things from time to time, but she's obstinate too and she usually sticks to them. I'd be interested to find out what caused this change of mind.'

'Probably, she was just stunned with shock when she gave the first version, and back in her right mind again after eight hours sleep and a hearty breakfast.'

'That remains to be seen. In the meantime, we have other matters nearer home to occupy us. You are about to meet the celebrated Helena and Little Sir Echo Ritchie.'

'Am I? I was rather hoping to get in a round of golf before lunch.'

'Get it in this afternoon, if you don't mind awfully. Helena has a great contempt for our police force, so it's high time she met a handsome, civilised specimen like yourself, to convert her.'

'Why has she got such a down on us? Any particular reason, in her case, I mean?'

'I don't know. Mrs Parkes says it all comes from reading the wrong newspaper, but I should imagine there might be more to it than that, wouldn't you? It would be nice to think that she'd been in a little trouble with them at some point. Better still, of course, if her dislike was based on the fear of their finding out something she would prefer them not to know.'

'Like the day when she substituted aspirin for Aunt Myrtle's digitalis, for instance? Or have you now abandoned your crossword puzzle?'

'No, I'm still at it. In fact, Joyce's accident has opened up another new corner. It is rather fun, particularly since it didn't end fatally.'

'Correct me if I'm wrong, but I assume the clues in this section point to the fact that she either knew, or was getting close to finding out, who killed Gwen, and as a result had been moved up to second place on the murderer's list. Realising this, her best hope of safety lay in playing it dumb and pretending to believe that her fall was accidental and not associated with any human agency.'

'No, you are not wrong. That could easily be the answer.'

'And you seriously expect her to admit to you what she has, understandably, been so assiduous in concealing from the police?'

'Not seriously, no. In fact, that wouldn't really suit me. What I hope to do is confront her with some statements, naming names as I go along, which she will deny with as much vehemence as is compatible with sparing my feelings and living up to her headmistress's precepts. While she is doing that, I shall be keeping a watch on the fingers of her left hand.'

'Harbingers of bad news is becoming our role,' I told Helena, refilling her glass for the second time, a duty which the host had been notably lax in performing. 'And here comes some more of it, I'm afraid. You may not have heard yet about Joyce?'

She did not, as I had been half prepared for, ask me who Joyce was. The combined effects of wine from a decent vineyard and the ardent attention accorded to her by Robin, as he listened dutifully to her warbling on about the erosions to human rights which beset us on all sides, had put her in a mellow mood and toned down the more aggressive side of her self-castigation.

'Joyce Harman, you mean? No, I hadn't. She's not ill, I hope?'

'No, only a bit bruised and generally knocked about. She fell down at the Green Park underground station yesterday afternoon.'

'Fell down? On to the line, you mean?'

'Not quite, luckily. That could have happened, but someone grabbed her in the nick of time.'

'Poor woman! What a dreadful thing! But she wasn't badly hurt, you say?'

'Nothing serious. It was mainly shock.'

'I should think so, indeed! What on earth can she have been doing in Piccadilly on a Saturday afternoon. Certainly not shopping at that time of day.'

'God knows. Lunching next door at the Ritz, maybe?'

'Who, Joyce? My dear, we must be talking about two different . . . Oh, I see, that was meant to be a joke. How stupid of me! You consider the idea to be as far fetched as I do. Hardly the sort of ambience one associates with someone like her, is it?' Helena asked, evidently bent on explaining my joke to me. 'Quite honestly, one finds it hard to picture Joyce having any sort of social life. She always seemed to have so few interests outside the Montgomerie clan. Such a pathetic, arid life, I always felt. Still, one is bound to admit that she has always been definitely rather peculiar, so I daresay that claustrophobic, hothouse world was the only one she could have survived in. One dreads to think what her life must have become now. Not surprising if she's going about in a sort of daze. It's probably not safe for her to be out on her own at all, let alone on the tube.'

This was hardly the impression I had gained myself, but she seemed as eager to talk about Joyce as I was to listen, so I did not spoil things by arguing, but asked instead:

'Have you seen anything of her lately?'

'Oh, my dear, don't remind me, I beg you! I feel awful enough as it is. I've been so terribly selfish and neglectful. I knew I ought to do something . . . get in touch with her after that dreadful business with Gwen. I meant to, but you know how it is? So many lame ducks, all making their demands on one's precious time. Curiously enough, though, I had a letter from poor Joyce only the other day, which made me feel worse than ever.'

'Was she writing to condole about your aunt's death?'

'Oh, no, no, that was weeks ago. This was something quite different. To tell you the truth, I didn't take it very seriously at the time. I thought, well, you know, the shock of Gwen's death had really unhinged her for the time being and that the best thing was to ignore it and hope she'd come round to a more sensible point of view. Now, of course, I can see that I was probably at fault there. If I'd only taken a more positive attitude and looked a little deeper below the surface, who knows, I might somehow have been able to prevent this . . . so called accident.'

'You are not suggesting, by any chance, that this so called accident might have been attempted suicide?'

'Well, do you find that so far fetched? Oh, please tell me you do! I can't swear that I should be wholly convinced, but at least it might raise a doubt and take some of the burden off my wretched conscience.'

'Frankly, Helena, I find it almost impossible to tell you anything at all, since I have no idea what her letter was about.'

'Oh, did I not tell you? How stupid of me! Head somewhere up there in the clouds, as usual, and I'm afraid I'm always at my least down to earth when it comes to money matters.'

'Money? Do you mean she wrote and asked you to lend her some money?'

'Oh heavens, no, if only she had! That wouldn't have presented the slightest difficulty, but it was the other way round, I'm sorry to say. It was about a legacy she'd had from my aunt, you see. She left Joyce five hundred pounds and some little trinket, of no particular value, I understand, but which Joyce had always admired. The letter was to say that she proposed to keep this as a memento, but would be writing to the solicitors to tell them that she couldn't accept the money.'

'Why not?'

'I'm afraid it shows how far her mind was wandering, poor dear. Her explanation was that she felt that, far from Aunt Myrtle owing her anything, the boot was on the other foot. She had received nothing but kindness from her during her lifetime and she did not feel entitled to any rewards. Isn't that incredible? Quite unbalanced, of course, and I could kick myself now for not recognising the signs.'

'I don't see why, though, Helena. It was certainly an unusual reaction, I grant you, but I wouldn't have called it an indication of insanity or melancholia.'

'But then perhaps you are not a deeply intuitive person? I have always liked to believe that I do possess some small gift in that direction, but, if so, it has certainly let me down this time and I must be more on the alert in future.'

It was becoming clear that it now suited Helena to believe that Joyce had tried to commit suicide, that she was largely to blame for it and, furthermore, that she was beginning to revel in the whole new field it opened up for self-reproach. It was therefore a favourable moment for further probing and I asked:

'Did she have any suggestions about what should be done with the money?'

'Oh, indeed, and that was another thing which put me on the wrong track. It was all so cut and dried. She said she realised there might be some legal difficulty in returning the money to the estate and so she considered the best solution would be to give it to some charity, to be decided on by myself and the executors. I ask you! Do you wonder that I didn't take it seriously? After all, if that's what she genuinely wanted, why not have given it to a charity herself?'

'Unless,' I suggested, 'she thought that, if she didn't deserve the money, then neither did she deserve the honour and glory of giving it away?'

'You over-estimate her, my dear. I still see it as a manifestation of severe mental disturbance and I have quite made up my mind that I must somehow find the time to get in touch with her and see if there's any way I can help.'

If she had made up her mind, there was no point in warning her of what she might be letting herself in for, so I changed the subject and soon afterwards she called Ritchie to heel and, having put her head round the kitchen door to say a grovelling word of farewell to Mrs Parkes, walked arm in arm with him back across the garden to White Gables.

'You did marvels with Helena,' I told Robin, 'I have never seen her so mellow. How did you get on with Ritchie?'

'Oh, I did marvels with him too. At least I hope so, because I put a lot into it and I have learnt far more than I ever wished to know about abstract art. I also had to sit through a comprehensive report on their visit to the Summer Exhibition.'

'Don't tell me they've hung one of Helena's ghastly pictures?' Toby asked.

'No, no, I should think not, indeed. She wouldn't demean herself by submitting one. In fact, I think yesterday's tour must have been a form of sadomasochism. They wanted to be shocked and scandalised by ninety per cent of the exhibits and their wish was granted. They managed to find something cruel to say about practically all of them.'

'Where is the Summer Exhibition?' I asked.

'At Burlington House, of course, exactly where it has always been for these past two hundred summers.'

'Oh yes, that's right, in Piccadilly. How very convenient!'

'Convenient for whom, I wonder?'

'Oh well, you know, Toby, for Ritchie and Helena, of course. In case they felt like nipping across for a carrot salad at the Ritz afterwards.'

20

'Oh, how lovely! Aren't they gorgeous? My favourite, too. But you shouldn't, you know. I'm not ill or anything.'

'That's all right. People are not supposed to mind getting flowers just because they're feeling well.'

'Oh well, no, that's true . . . probably enjoy them all the more. Can you . . . er . . . come in for a minute? Or perhaps you're dashing off somewhere and in a tearing hurry?'

'No, not specially. I'd love to come in and talk to you for a minute.'

'Oh, good! I can even offer you a drink. The only snag is. . . .'

'What?'

'Well, I was just thinking, if you'd come in your car, it might be a bit tricky leaving it outside. You're not really allowed to park in this street unless you have one of those special permits.'

'No, that's all right too, I came by taxi.'

'Oh, I see. Oh well, in that case, let's go and sit down then.'

It was not the most enthusiastic welcome I had ever received, but I did not attribute her reluctance to the balance of her mind being disturbed. I considered it more likely, in view of the shabby, linoleum covered staircase I had climbed to reach her attic apartment and the chipped and battered old refrigerator which stood beside us on the landing, that she feared I would despise her dingy surroundings. If so, she had some justification, for the bedsitter, with its screened-in wash basin in one corner and electric hot plate in another, although clean and orderly as a hospital ward five minutes before matron was due on her rounds, was also just about as negative and impersonal.

'Do sit down,' Joyce said, pointing to the only chair in the room which had any pretensions to comfort and then drawing aside a section of the screen. 'I'll just stick these in the basin for now and arrange them later,' giving rise to the thought that a pot plant might have been a more tactful offering.

'Would you like some champagne?' she

asked when she had disposed of the flowers.

'My goodness, Joyce, what's this then? Are you celebrating your deliverance from the jaws of London Transport?'

'Well, we could, you know. I've had another visitor today. He brought me a bottle of champagne. Two half bottles, I should say.'

'What a sensible man! But don't open one for me. Keep them for a day when you're not feeling quite so well.'

'I don't have to open it. He did that while he was here. He opened one of them and said that now I would have to drink it, whether I wanted to or not, otherwise it would be a wicked waste.'

'How true! And in that case, I think we should lose no time.'

'It's in the refrigerator,' she said, getting up.

'Oh yes, of course, your refrigerator.'

'I have to keep it on the landing. There isn't really room for it in here and besides, it makes rather a funny noise sometimes.'

She was away for several minutes, which I spent on an inspection of the bookshelves, having heard that they can provide valuable insights into the owner's character. It did

277

not tell me much that I had not already learnt or guessed, however. There were a number of tattered old guide books, mostly about Greece or Arabia, quite a comprehensive collection of the works of Angela Brazil and more than a dozen bound copies of a magazine called *Little Folks*.

There was also a section devoted to Montgomerie memorabilia. Two of the shelves here contained copies of what I assumed to have been his entire literary output and above and below them were text books and encyclopaedias on subjects relating to criminal law and forensic science. I concluded that, as well as typing all his books and being at the beck and call of both his wives, Joyce had done most of his research.

When she returned she was carrying a tray containing two large tumblers, each about one third full, plus the bottle with the same amount still left in it.

'I am afraid these are not quite the right glasses,' she said, in case I hadn't noticed.

'Oh, never mind,' I replied, taking a sip from mine, 'I expect it will taste just as good.'

As a matter of fact, it did not taste just as

good. It was ice cold, but flat as tap water, which may have been the explanation, and there was also the possibility that she had placed it beside something in the refrigerator which had a very pungent smell. So I put my glass down and turned my attention to the label on the bottle.

'Your visitor did you proud,' I remarked. 'He obviously holds you in high regard.'

'Who, Jim? No, he doesn't, not at all.'

'Jim Temple?'

'Yes, that's right. It was very kind of him to bring it, but he doesn't hold me in high regard. It was just part of the prescribed treatment. He said something about champagne being a good tonic and soothing to the nerves.'

'I thought his speciality was heart disease, not neurology?'

'So it is, but that wouldn't make any difference. It was Helena who sent him, you see. She's got the idea that I've gone a bit batty. I suppose she wouldn't want to get mixed up in anything like that herself, so she asked Jim to come instead.'

'Did he tell you so?'

'Well . . . no . . . not exactly, but I sort of got it out of him. I asked him how he knew I'd . . . had this stupid fall and he said Helena had told him and she was very worried about me.'

'You astonish me, Joyce. I seem to have got everything badly mixed up. I was under the impression that Jim was Ritchie's friend, not Helena's.'

'Oh well, I daresay he is now, but if so I should think it must have been through Helena that they met. She and Jim were always at South Park Terrace in the old days. They were two of a kind, in a way. We all used to think . . . well . . . that they . . . Myrtle made a great joke of it afterwards. Jim was her godson, you know. She said that Ritchie only married Helena to restore her self-esteem when Jim ditched her and after a year or two her self-esteem had grown so fat and greedy that it had eaten him up and spat him out. She used to say outrageous things like that sometimes.'

'It seems to run in the family,' I remarked, 'only Helena's outrageous things aren't usually so sharp. So Jim's never married?'

'No, never.'

'Perhaps he would have, eventually, if Gwen were still alive?'

'I don't know.'

'You've gone very quiet, Joyce, and you haven't touched your champagne. Is there something wrong with it?'

'No, I was . . . waiting for you.'

She was sitting perfectly still, with her hands folded in her lap, in her little low slung chair, and all at once I felt like a headmistress, powerful and impregnable behind my imposing desk, and heard my voice sounding gentle and patronising, as I said:

'Or have you, by any chance, forgotten which glass the dose is in? If so, it might be best if neither of us were to drink any. After all, you never know, you might not be so lucky next time.'

21

'Poor old Joyce, she really was an incurable
liar,' I remarked, 'but she was no fool and
she wasn't a coward either. She pursued her
relentless, private crusade to the bitter end
and when something went wrong she was
very resourceful about turning it to her own
advantage. She had one serious weakness,
though, which let her down from time to
time.'

'Like an unfortunate tendency to kill off
anyone who incurred her disapproval?' Toby
suggested, having agreed to spend the evening with us at Beacon Square, so that he
could hear my reconstruction of events leading to the murder of Gwen Montgomerie.

'No, I was still thinking about the way
she lied. Often her speech was so hesitant
and jumbled as to make it hard to grasp
what she was on about, but whenever she
was lying she became much more fluent and

articulate. For example, when she was telling me how completely broken up Gwen was by Willie's death and how her life had become so empty that her only solace came from spending long hours at the hairdresser, it all came reeling out as though it had been rehearsed. It was a trick which after a while became easy to recognise and it's no wonder that she always got caught out at school. Towards the end, when I was beginning to get her character sorted out, it was no longer a question of whether she had been lying about a certain point, but why.'

'Does this mean,' Robin asked, 'that Joyce had known all along that the hairdresser was a blind and that Gwen had found quite a different way of consoling herself during Willie's absences?'

'I'm afraid so, and that's what started her off on the downward path. She fooled me there at first, I must admit. If you remember, Toby, I told you that, since she didn't give a damn about her own appearance and her hair was always such a mess, she probably couldn't tell the difference between a home wash and a professional one?'

'Yes, so you did.'

'A foolish mistake, if ever there was one.

She was listening and observing the whole time and very little slipped past her. Mr Banks put that into words for me the first time the three of us met. He was panting for a drink and Joyce told him about a pub just down the road from the crematorium. "The things you know, Joyce!" he said and he obviously wasn't being sarcastic. I expect he automatically assumed that Willie had taken her there on some similar outing and the pub and its exact location had been registered in her memory for all time. He made a similar comment about her when I met him again last week, and thinking about that afterwards, I realised how right he was and how stupid of me not to have paid more attention the first time.'

'Oh, don't flog yourself to death with self-reproaches,' Toby said, 'it's not your style and you're beginning to sound like Helena.'

'Besides, you're not doing too badly,' Robin added, 'if you really believe you have found a connection between Gwen's affair with Jim Temple and her subsequent murder. Not to mention I suppose the demise of Willie and Myrtle, as well?'

'Yes, in a sense, I think I have. Not that

I ever doubted, as you know, that Willie died from natural causes. Joyce did, though. As Nigel Banks also pointed out, she noticed everything and remembered everything, but having no first hand experience of life, she sometimes drew the wrong conclusions from what she had seen and heard. She must have been demented with misery when Willie died, rather unexpectedly as you'll remember, and it was knowing all about Gwen's secret life, combined with the fact that Jim was a doctor, which planted the idea that, between them, they had somehow contrived to bring about or, at the very least, hasten his death. It was made all the easier to believe, I might add, by its close resemblance to an incident in Myrtle's manuscript, which had been lying around on the premises for several months, for anyone to pick up and read. Anyway, from that moment she began to work out her vengeance, although I should explain that it did not include murder at this stage. She only resorted to that when she was driven to it, and the original plan was much more subtle and imaginative. She would fashion a double-edged sword, with which to cut down Myrtle and Gwen with a single swipe.'

'And a very picturesque analogy, if I may say so, but what had poor old Myrtle done to deserve such treatment?'

'Oh, plenty, Toby, you may be sure. She was worse than Gwen, in her way. So far as Joyce was concerned, each of the women Willie loved had two sides to her. She was a threat and an intruder, simply because he did love her, but, being necessary to his well-being, so long as he was alive, she was someone to be cherished and protected. Myrtle was the extreme case. As well as being unfaithful to Willie during their marriage, it was she who finally left him. In addition to that, she had dared to become a celebrity in her own right and, to crown it all, he continued to adore her, even after they parted. Can you imagine a more damning record? I don't suppose it was made any easier to bear by the fact that she was so good natured and generous and that, in any other circumstances, Joyce would have adored her too.'

'What was this weapon you spoke of?' Robin asked, 'and how did she use it?'

'Oh well, you know the answer to that one, we all do. Let me first of all remind you that Joyce did all Willie's secretarial work, correspondence included, and that he had complete trust in her. Therefore, no one would have known better than she the sad history of Myrtle's clairvoyance and the trouble it had brought on her. She also knew that Willie had been unable to read her last novel before he died. So she removed the manuscript from the rest of his papers, swore to Myrtle, with one hand on her heart and the other tapping out a tune, that she had never set eyes on it, and set about using one chapter from it for her own ends. You both know what happened next.'

There was a short silence and then Robin said: 'You really mean to tell us that Joyce was the evil genius behind that plot to steal Myrtle's work?'

'Certainly, I do. Gwen would never have had the wits or daring to devise such a scheme. Nor would she have had the least idea how to carry it out, without Joyce to organise everything, including more or less writing the script herself. The original was largely in dialogue form anyway, and she'd worked with Willie on every one of his novels, not to mention six episodes of a television script, so she was perfectly capable of doing an adaptation job of that kind.'

'All the same,' Toby said, 'that is not really quite my idea of a really spiteful revenge. It was, after all, Gwen who was going to get the credit, and the money too, presumably. Or did they mean to share that between them?'

'Oh, no. In theory, Gwen was to sit back and collect the rewards, while Joyce did all the work. Those had always been their roles, so there was nothing unnatural about it, and you can see how easily Gwen would have been persuaded to play her part. Here was all that valuable property being scooped up into the archives, just for the benefit of biographers and essayists and any old university student who took a fancy to write a thesis. Whereas the poor, indigent widow was hardly able to scrape up the money for the supermarket. Naturally, Joyce didn't bother to explain that Willie hadn't written a word of this one and that it didn't belong in the archives. She told Gwen, drumming her fingers, no doubt, as she spoke, that if it succeeded this time they could pull off the same trick again.'

'I begin to get the drift now,' Robin said. 'That's what Joyce told her, but she didn't mean it?'

'Not one word. Sooner or later the whole sordid truth would have come out. Joyce would have seen to that and then Gwen would have been humiliated and disgraced, most of all in the eyes of the very people she had fought so long to get accepted by. But the later the better of course, and the higher the climb the harder the fall. A fine revenge, don't you agree?'

'Yes, and you must forgive me for continually harping on the same note, but I still can't understand why it then became necessary for Gwen to be murdered?'

'I hope to make that clear in a minute, but first of all, to keep everything in its proper sequence, we must return to Myrtle.'

'Ah yes, poor Myrtle!' Toby said. 'But at least for her it was a case of sooner rather than later. She must have snuffed out from her heart attack before she even realised how she was being victimised. A truly merciful release, one might say.'

'On the contrary, Toby, it was precisely the discovery of how she was being victimised which led to the heart attack and the snuffing.'

289

'Oh, I see. Or do I? No, I'm not sure that I do.'

'We all assumed, although I am not quite sure why, that the telephone was off the hook because she had been trying to call for help, but it was the other way round. What had happened was that someone had called her, to pass on some news of so shocking a nature that it led directly, almost instantaneously, to a fatal attack.'

'The someone being Joyce?'

'Yes, though I don't for one moment believe she had intended the revelation to come so soon, or to have such a catastrophic effect. She would have preferred it to come by degrees, for Myrtle to have suffered the slow torment of discovering how she was being tricked and defrauded and the realisation that there was nothing she could do to stop it.'

'Why not?' Toby asked. 'She was a woman of spirit by all accounts, and I can see her making a damn good try at stopping it.'

'It wouldn't have been any use. She didn't possess so much as a rough draft of the typescript she had sent to Willie and it would simply have been her word against

290

theirs. Joyce had only to announce that no such document had ever existed, or, if it had, Willie had never received it, and everyone would have believed her. She was dull, dependable old Joyce, who had never had an axe to grind in her life and Myrtle . . . well, it was well known that Myrtle had lost her touch and her talent and fallen out of the race years ago. How sad that she should now have become paranoiac about it and was going round, spreading these wild claims about plagiarism! Oh no, Myrtle wouldn't have stood a chance.'

Robin said:

'But you haven't explained why, if Joyce hadn't intended to deliver the knock-out blow so early in the proceedings, she then changed her mind?'

'It wasn't deliberate. I am sure she had no idea that one telephone call would do the trick. Indeed, how could she? But it was at this point that her plans had started to crumble very slightly round the edges and she had to act quickly. Nothing serious, you understand, but a new element had crept in, which she hadn't bargained for.'

'What new element?'

'Well, to put it bluntly, Robin, it was you.'

'Me? Oh no, Tessa, you can't blame me for anything. What could I have done?'

'Turned up at the Alibi Club dinner, that's what. You, the up and coming young star from Scotland Yard. Joyce would have heard all about your being the guest of honour, if not from Myrtle then certainly from Gwen and possibly Nigel Banks as well. She would also have heard how Myrtle had made a point of coming up to talk to us, how I'd been to lunch with her a week later and how she was to dine with us on the following Sunday. Joyce didn't care for it at all and she must have been haunted by the fear that matters were slipping out of her control. So she had to do something drastic to halt the drift. As I say, I don't suppose she had the least expectation that the short, sharp shock she delivered over the telephone would finish Myrtle off, but she must have hoped that it would at least lay her out for the evening, if not for several weeks, and would certainly put paid to her coming to dinner with us. Poor Joyce, I expect she felt badly about it afterwards and that's why she returned the five hundred pounds.'

'Her legacy, you mean?'

'Yes, she told Helena that she would be sending it back. There was also a ruby brooch, if you remember, but she could hardly return that as well. It would have been too absurd and Helena would have had her certified on the spot. However, she had her principles you know, and she had no intention of hanging on to it. Last Saturday afternoon, in a crowded underground station, just as the train was coming in, she tried to chuck the brooch on to the line.'

'Tried to?'

'I daresay anyone else would have managed it without any trouble, but I've often told you how clumsy and unco-ordinated she was, and in taking the brooch out of her bag, she dropped it on the platform. When she bent down to pick it up she lost her balance and almost went over the edge herself. Someone hauled her back and also, as you know, retrieved the brooch. She got his name and address from the police constable who interviewed her at the hospital and posted it to him, in gratitude for saving her life. Poor Joyce, I can't help feeling sorry for her. She was a strange woman and no mistake, but she wasn't a fool and she wasn't a coward and she did sacrifice her whole life to other people. Still, I daresay she won't mind being in prison as much as most people would. I expect they'll be able to put her in charge of the library or something and, in a way, it will be rather like being back at her boarding school again.'

'I'll decide whether to feel sorry for her or not,' Robin said, 'when you've answered the final question, and you know what that is.'

'Gwen, you mean? Well, without wishing to boast, I do think I can take some of the credit for that.'

'No one ever wishes to boast,' Toby said, 'they find they are doing it despite themselves, and I am not sure that credit is quite the right word in this context.'

'Blame, then, if you must be pedantic. There I was, you see, pressing on relentlessly with my campaign to reinstate Myrtle's reputation and Joyce could tell that I didn't mean to give up. She'd already been forced to drop a warning hint to Gwen and Gwen was getting worried sick. She was sleeping badly and spending more and more time stocking up with mountains of stuff she didn't need from the supermarket. Joyce realised that the breaking point was not far off and that she must act quickly. For Gwen to have broken down and given the game away before the television programme went out would have ruined the whole plan and left Joyce as the one with egg on her face. It would also have made a mockery of her whole life and so Gwen had to go.'

'Well, all right, but how the hell was it done and how did she manage to get away with it?'

'Oh, simple! She was staying in the house that night, you see. It wouldn't have been difficult to make an excuse to do that because there was a small bedroom which had always been set aside for her. She kept some of her belongings there. So there was never any fuss or bother if, for some reason, it became necessary for her to spend the night. I told you that Gwen was getting worried and nervous and was sleeping badly and one of her panaceas was to go down during the night to make herself a hot drink. So all Joyce had to do was station herself behind the kitchen door and then, when the moment came, wham, bash! Out goes she!'

'But what about the weapon? What did she use and what became of it?'

'Oh yes, that old weapon! What a stunt! And one can't really blame the police. They did their best, but how were they to know that by the time they came on the scene it had already been melted down to less than half its original size?'

'Melted, did you say?'

'That's right. It was your telling me that it must have been something like a sledge-hammer which did the trick.'

'I can't imagine how.'

'Well, you see, in the next breath you mentioned that there'd been a hammer in the kitchen tool box and it just so happened that not long afterwards I read a magazine article about how to make strange and useless objects out of ice. Perhaps Joyce had read it too. Anyway, one of the things you were supposed to do was to make a bowl look as though it had been carved out of a block of ice and serve your fruit salad in it on hot summer days and so forth. What you had to do was to put one glass bowl inside a larger one with enough water in it to come up to the rim of both, and then put the whole contraption into the freezer. When the water had turned to ice you took it out again, thawed the outside of the bigger bowl in warm water and, hey presto, out comes the inner bowl, which has now grown an inch or two thicker all the way round and appears to be cut from solid ice. Quite neat, really, if you could be bothered, and it made me realise that by working on the same principle, so long as you left the handle exposed, you could transform an ordinary domestic hammer into something three or four times its original size and weight. The great charm of course being that, once it had done its job, it would revert to its original form simply by being held under the hot tap for two minutes and even the most brilliant forensic scientist in the whole world could never find one shred of evidence to show that it had been used to smash someone's skull in. The whole operation could have been accomplished in less than ten minutes, starting from the moment when Joyce heard sounds from Gwen's bedroom, or saw the staircase light come on, and then as soon as it was daylight she set off for Notting Hill, not forgetting, of course, to smash a basement window on her way out.'

'Did she tell you all this herself?'

'Oh yes, and a lot of other things when

we had our little chat, after she'd made a feeble attempt to dope my drink, as a first step to polishing me off as well. Poor old Joyce, she made a proper botch of that one, but of course she was getting desperate by then. I can't help feeling sorry about it. It does so madden me, you know, that someone so intrinsically good as Joyce should come such a cropper, while fakes and hypocrites like Helena get away with absolutely everything. Except murder, of course.'

'Then I have reassuring news for you,' Toby said. 'Helena has had her come-uppance, or come-downance might be a better description, and White Gables is up for sale again.'

'No! You don't mean it? Has she now committed a murder, or has the call of Blackheath proved too strong?'

'Neither. Ritchie, I must tell you, had been despatched on a mission to the third world, but when he arrived at Heathrow airport there was a message to say that the President of the country he was proposing to visit had been ousted in a military coup and the trip was cancelled.'

'And so?'

'And so he returned to White Gables in

the early hours to find his close friend and former deputy in residence and pyjamas, if not flagrante. The worm then did a U turn and stamped out again, saying that they would be hearing from his solicitors.'

'Fancy that! So now we know how Helena spent all those evenings in London, when Ritchie thought she was taking Aunt Myrtle to the Festival Hall. I am so glad to have that point cleared up at last and I think it's all absolutely splendid.'

'I knew you would be pleased. Mrs Parkes, I need hardly say, is disgusted. Not on moral grounds, you may rest assured, nor even because Helena had dared to insult her intelligence by saying that the close friend and former deputy was her cousin from Canada. She had always liked to believe that people in our neighbourhood conduct their affairs, both illicit and otherwise, with more finesse. She associates this kind of outré behaviour more readily with places like Maidenhead.'

'Quite right too and I consider Roakes Common to be well rid of them. I wonder who you'll get there next?'

'I don't know, but they could hardly be worse, do you think, Robin?'

'I'm not so sure about that. They could be, I suppose.'

'In what way?'

'Well, they might have children or dogs. On the other hand, they could be thoroughly upright, intrinsically good, impeccably mannered people, who just happened to have committed a murder or two. And you can guess what that would lead to, I daresay?'

The publishers hope that this Large Print Book has brought you pleasurable reading. Each title is designed to make the text as easy to see as possible. G.K. Hall Large Print Books are available from your library and your local bookstore. Or you can receive information on upcoming and current Large Print Books by mail and order directly from the publisher. Just send your name and address to:

G.K. Hall & Co.
70 Lincoln Street
Boston, Mass. 02111

or call, toll-free:

1-800-343-2806

A note on the text
Large print edition designed by
Bernadette Montalvo.
Composed in 16 pt. Plantin
on a Xyvision 300/Linotron 202N
by Genevieve Connell
of G.K. Hall & Co.